COUNTRY PROPOSAL

A SWEET ROMANCE

CAROLYNE AARSEN

Misty Ridge
Publishing

To Second Chances

I'd like to thank Hannah Linder from hannahlinderdesigns.com for her amazing work on the cover of this book and the other Millars Crossing books.

I also want to thank my husband for his support and encouragement through my entire writing career.

CHAPTER ONE

"I know you have an agenda," Finn grumbled as he set the plant pots Katrina gave him in the back of his truck. "Wyatt or Reuben could easily have delivered these to Etta."

His future sister-in-law gave him a patronizing pat on the shoulder and shook her head. "You're far too suspicious. You've got to stop judging people by your standards."

"I have high standards." Finn brushed the dirt off the front of his pants and slammed the tailgate of his truck, now parked in front of Katrina's greenhouse. He'd come to town to pick up some minerals, milk replacer, and vitamin shots for the calves when he got Katrina's text asking if he would do her a favor.

He couldn't say no, given their renter, Etta Caprice, lived on the way to the ranch.

More importantly, Etta was single.

He shot Katrina another suspicious glance, but her smile was wide and innocent. Not that that meant anything. He'd known

Katrina since the day she'd come to Millars Crossing as a young teen. She had her devious moments and wasn't averse to unsubtle matchmaking.

"It was those superior standards that made me realize you're the perfect man for the job," Katrina said, flashing him a broad grin. "I knew you would do it proficiently and with a smile."

"I'm not sure about the smile, but I can handle proficient."

"Don't be such a bear," Katrina chided. "We're trying to be neighborly and friendly."

"Etta's lived in that house for the last month and a half. Why so friendly now?"

"I've been friendly since she came here. I just need these plants delivered. I'm getting rid of the last of my stock and I could use your help."

Now she sounded snippy, which made Finn feel like a heel.

"Okay, but that's all I'm doing. Delivering these pots and heading back to the ranch."

"I'm not asking you to take her out for lunch." She shook her head as if she couldn't believe the stubbornness of her future brother-in-law. "It's just being a good neighbor. No different from when Reuben went there to fix her taps."

"And he tried hard to get me to do that too," Finn grumbled.

Katrina shook her head, frowning. "What's gotten into you?" she asked. "You're such a grump."

Finn shrugged, not sure what to tell her, surprised she noticed. He thought he'd kept his feelings hidden. The last couple weeks he had been out of sorts. He enjoyed working on the ranch, but lately felt empty. Lonely.

Which was surprising, considering how many people hung out at the ranch.

His sister Carly had moved a fifth-wheel trailer onto the property and was living in it. Her building permit for the event center she wanted to build on the ranch had been approved, so she was going full tilt on that. Even as he stood grumbling to

Katrina, the construction crew was already on site, trenching water and power lines and setting up grade beams in the coming week.

He and Reuben shared the old house their parents had lived in before they built the large rambling ranch house that Wyatt and his three children now lived in, so he didn't spend much time alone. Everyone ate together in the big house when they could. And they would until Adele and Wyatt got married in September and Adele moved in. Then, she had announced to all the Sutton siblings, they were on their own.

When they got married, Reuben and Katrina would move to a new acreage that had recently been subdivided off the main quarter section. Katrina was expanding her greenhouse and landscaping business and growing her own stock on that land.

Everyone had a plan and a purpose. And though he was working his way into the ranch and happy to be home, a restlessness still gripped him.

"Maybe I need to plan another trip?" He threw the question out as a joke, but from the way Katrina narrowed her eyes, he guessed she didn't see the humor.

"You're not seriously considering that?" she asked, her frown deepening.

Finn held up his hands in a gesture of defense. "Down, girl," he chided. "I was kidding."

"Well, that's good," Katrina said. "Reuben and Wyatt count on you being around."

"I wouldn't leave them in the lurch," he said. "I've become more responsible."

He made a show of pulling out his phone and glancing at it. "And I better get going. I have things to do today."

Katrina seemed to relax. "Say hi to Etta for me. Tell her she can come down to the ranch anytime."

"And do what?" Finn asked.

"You could take her horseback riding."

3

He wasn't taking that bait. "Gotta run," was all he said, tossing off another wave, getting into his truck, and driving away.

He had to drive slowly because of the plants in the back, but he didn't mind. Warm sunshine poured out of the sky, and it was great to have time to himself.

He'd been traveling for the past four years. He told his brothers it was to get away from Millars Crossing and bad memories. But the novelty of traveling, seeing fresh places, soon paled. A near-death experience gave him a reset.

So, he came back to Millars Crossing.

Half an hour later, he pulled up to the house where Etta stayed. A few years ago, it had been the house where Reuben and his late wife, Denise, had lived.

The ramp Denise used for her walker still led to the front of the house.

Finn strolled up the ramp and knocked at the door. He waited, looking around the yard. Two weeks ago, Reuben and Katrina had come here to rake the lawn and weed the overgrown flowerbeds. Another job they had tried to foist onto him, but he had ducked that one also.

He didn't hear any noise coming from the house, so he knocked again. All the curtains were drawn, which meant he couldn't see if she was inside.

Her car was here. Maybe she was out for a walk.

He strolled down the ramp and back to the truck. He shifted the pots to the rear of the truck bed then took them out. Two went beside the door. Two at the foot of the ramp. The remaining pots he hung from brackets on either side of the door. The cheerful flowers added a delightful splash of color to the house.

Taking a chance, he knocked again.

This time the door opened. A tall, slender woman stepped out, her copper-colored hair pulled back in a messy topknot. Her loose white shirt and yoga pants held streaks of gray, white, and black paint. Her hazel eyes, fringed with thick lashes, looked at him with an appraising look. As if she had judged and found him wanting.

It rankled because he didn't understand why she would look at him that way. They had only met in passing at the grocery store when Finn did a run for Wyatt's nanny.

"Good morning. Sorry to intrude. Katrina wanted me to bring you these," he said, flipping his hand toward the pots on the deck. "Said it would brighten your day."

Her features relaxed into a slow smile.

Which created a curl of attraction and appeal.

"Thanks. That was sweet of her," Etta said.

"Yeah, she's a great girl."

Silence followed his comment, and Finn wondered how soon he could leave without looking rude.

Etta cleared her throat just as he was about to make his escape.

"Actually, now that you're here," she said, sounding apologetic, "I need some help. I'm having trouble with the AC unit on the furnace. It doesn't want to kick in. I'm just getting warm air through the ductwork."

Finn resisted the urge to glance at his watch. A cow had calved this morning and didn't have enough milk. Reuben would be waiting for the milk-replacer he had bought. But his brother would also not want him to leave Etta in the lurch.

"I don't know much about AC. How about I have a quick look for now," he said.

"Okay. That sounds good."

She turned and without looking back to see if he followed her, walked into the house. She looked as good going as coming, he thought.

Part of him didn't want to be interested. It would only play into Katrina's nefarious plans, and yet he had to admit she was attractive.

"If you don't mind, I'll check the thermostat first," he said.

"That's fine, it's down the hall."

"I know where it is," he said. "I used to come and visit Denise and Reuben when they lived here."

"I understand Reuben is your brother?"

"Not that he would want to admit it, but yeah, he is." Finn moved past her into the kitchen and then down the hall.

Though it had been two years since his sister-in-law Denise died, he felt a twinge of sorrow created by the memories in this house. Though her and Reuben's marriage was far from happy, Denise had still been an old friend from school.

"So, the thermostat is turned way down, like it should be." He fiddled with the gauge. As he turned it up, he heard the furnace kick in.

"Sounds like that part works," he said. "Let me just check the air coming through the ductwork, if you don't mind."

She nodded, and he walked to the room off the kitchen. He found a duct and felt warm air flowing out.

"Can you turn it down now?" he asked her.

She left, and he waited, but the temperature of the air didn't change. Finally, the furnace turned off.

"I'll check the unit in the basement," he said, pushing to his feet. As he stood, he saw a painting hanging on the wall where a bright and colorful landscape used to be.

Dark trees loomed over a gray pond. He glimpsed something reflected in the water. A face?

At any rate, it looked dark and dismal. Denise would not have approved.

He walked past Etta, who stood in the kitchen, washing some paintbrushes.

At the bottom of the stairs leading to the basement, he saw several canvases leaning against the wall and stopped to have a closer look at the first one. It depicted an early evening sky with a moon illuminating some clouds. It was skillfully painted but unwelcoming.

He heard Etta coming down the stairs behind him.

"I'm guessing you painted these and the one above the fireplace?" he asked.

"Yes. I did," she said.

He tilted his head one side, then another, wishing he hadn't drawn attention to the paintings. Another painting stood beside the first one he saw.

A large landscape in about seventy shades of gray and black. Dark, leafless trees silhouetted against a mottled gray sky. He could see she had talent, but the style didn't appeal to him. The one peeking from behind that one looked like the other three.

Depressing, he thought. He doubted she would appreciate the comment.

"They're interesting," he said, opting for an easy out.

"I'm sensing you don't like them." She spoke calmly, without challenge, which surprised him considering his vague word was worldwide code for *I don't like it, but I don't want to say that because my momma raised me to be polite,* and he guessed she knew it.

"Well…I don't know…" He tried to backpedal, knowing he'd been busted. "They're well done but—"

"Don't worry. They're not everyone's taste, but they've been well received by the college I hope to work for."

Again with that off-putting tone. As if she was tolerating him.

Which simultaneously grated and challenged him.

"There must be some depressed people working there." He was teasing her but as soon as the words left his mouth, he regretted them. Like he was insulting her art.

"I think some people need art to express emotions they don't

7

always know how to process. My paintings give them that outlet."

She looked at the painting as she spoke, but Finn saw a flicker of sadness pass over her features. He wondered what she had dealt with that made her want to express herself in such dark colors.

"Well, I'm more of a horses and mountains and blue skies kind of guy," he said, trying to lighten the atmosphere. "Do you ever paint those? Or flowers?"

She gave him a wry look that answered his question.

"Guess I won't be commissioning any work from you." Again, idiot. Something about this girl made him say dumb things.

"That would be a fair assessment," she said, her expression now deadpan. "Shall we look at the AC unit or do you want to talk about art more?"

He caught a challenging note in her voice but decided not to rise to the bait. Not hitting any home runs with her.

He followed her through the rest of the basement to where the furnace with its attached air conditioning unit sat.

The front panel had been removed and was set aside. "I know nothing about air conditioning units, but I thought maybe something might be dirty," was all she said as she stood aside for Finn.

He didn't know much about them either, but he knelt down to have a look. "Do you have a flashlight handy?"

She reached above him and handed him one.

He turned it on and shone it inside the unit. As far as he could tell everything looked normal. There were no leaks, no loose screws, and he didn't smell anything unusual. He flicked the flashlight off and stood, handing it back to her.

"I don't see anything I can help you with. I can call the HVAC guy for you."

"That would be great," she said. "It's been warm, and I'd love it if I could get the house cooled off."

He paused, frowning as he sniffed the air. "Does it usually smell this musty down here?"

"I don't know what's normal in this house."

"I'll ask Reuben."

She frowned at the furnace, tapping her fingers on her crossed arms. "Do you think something's wrong with the furnace instead?"

Finn just shrugged. "I can have a look at that too."

"That's okay. It's the air-conditioning that seems to be a problem."

She chewed one corner of her lip, looking concerned.

"Something else bothering you?"

"No? Why would you ask that?"

Definitely defensive, Finn thought. But he had done what he could. He had delivered the plants and he had looked at the air conditioner. His job here was finished.

"Well, in that case I should get a move on," he said. He walked past the paintings again, giving them another look. Still not feeling the love, but he paused anyway. "You might want to store these paintings somewhere else other than this basement. It's an older house and you never know what could happen."

Etta frowned as she seemed to consider this.

"I can give you a hand bringing them up," he said.

"No. I'll do that later."

He let it go. Her call and her paintings.

He walked up the stairs, Etta right behind him, and as he stepped outside into the sunshine, he felt as if a weight had dropped off his shoulders. It was weird. Like a heaviness lurked inside the house.

"Well, thanks for bringing the flowers," Etta said. "They look friendly."

"I'll call the repair guy. He can call you to arrange a time to come." Finn gave her another look, surprised again at the tug on his heart at the sight of her. But she wasn't looking at him.

"Thanks for your help," she said, then stepped into the house.

Probably going back to her dark and depressing paintings.

He shrugged off the thought, then shoved his hands in his pockets, whistling as he walked to the truck. It was a beautiful day. Life was great. Before he drove away, he glanced once more at the house. But Etta wasn't standing at the window looking at him.

So much for Katrina's matchmaking. This clearly would not work.

And yet, as he drove away, her easy dismissal of him wounded his pride.

❧

Etta dabbed more paint on the canvas then stood back. Her artist soul still fought with the comments Finn had made yesterday about her work.

Flowers and horses and blue skies indeed.

Monochrome was her brand, her style. What her art teacher had encouraged her to focus on. It was this work that had caught the attention of the Art Department of the college where she had applied for the artist-in-residence program. Getting that would be the coup she needed to, hopefully, get the tenured position she'd been aiming for ever since she started her arts degree. The position Alistair had groomed her for.

She jabbed her paintbrush in the swirl of gray and black paint she'd mixed on her palette, unintentionally spraying it on the canvas at the thought of her old art teacher.

Jerk.

Loser.

Two-Faced Liar.

And behind those accusations rose up an even more jarring one.

Trusting Idiot.

That last insult was for herself.

She had been a trusting idiot to fall for Alistair's lies and flattery. The entire time they were dating he told her that once she finished her degree and he was no longer her teacher they would get married.

Until then he needed to keep their relationship a secret, which hadn't been hard for Etta. At that bleak time in her life, after the death of her mother and after that, losing her brother, she had lost herself in her art and her studies. She kept to herself, making few friends. Which made it easy for Alistair to keep their relationship under wraps.

For five years she had clung to his promise of marriage. For five years she had made plans.

Until she found out he was married and had two children. Something he had kept conveniently to himself. Something, because of her isolation and the secrecy of their relationship, she knew nothing about.

She stabbed her brush at the canvas then immediately regretted her mini temper tantrum as the shadow she had been painstakingly creating was now the wrong shape. Stifling her frustration, she wiped off what she could, standing back to see if she could salvage what she had done. Loading her brush again, she continued, keeping her anger under control. She had come to this secluded place to build up her portfolio. To get away from Vancouver and all the stuff that haunted her there. The recriminations. The anger over Alistair's deceit.

The guilt.

She clenched her brush again, trying to find the place of peace she had found this morning before Finn came. She'd read her Bible, meditated, went for a walk. She needed to calm herself. To get herself into a place to finish her pieces. A lot was riding on getting them done to the best of her ability.

It hadn't helped that the AC didn't work. She was sweating as she worked despite having many of the windows in the house open. Trouble was she couldn't have the windows open in the room she was using as a studio because, as she had discovered, the wind whipped over the fields the room faced and brought dust inside.

But now, as it had yesterday, the sun beat into the room and she was getting hotter.

Even worse, she couldn't seem to get Finn and his comments off her mind. Like any artist, she struggled with feeling her work didn't measure up. She knew she was her own worst critic, but lately it had been difficult to work up enthusiasm for her projects.

And this particular work seemed especially elusive. This piece was the largest and would be the pièce de résistance of the entire showing she was putting together.

She had decided to split this canvas into four smaller canvases with a single painting spread out over all four. But she also wanted each canvas to stand on its own. This had proved challenging because once the entire piece was done, combined they would measure twenty feet wide by twenty feet high. Perspective had become the issue.

But now inspiration was harder to find.

She took a step back, looking from the canvas to the sketches she had made of each painting. Though she always made many preliminary sketches and, in this case, had made some smaller test canvases of the project, she often strayed from the original concept, letting artistic flow take over.

But today she wasn't feeling the flow. Actually, she hadn't felt the flow yesterday or the day before.

Life was interfering with her art.

Besides the AC not working, her car was at the mechanic's.

Apparently, something was wrong with the wheel bearings. And there was oil in the antifreeze which, she assumed, from the deep frown on the mechanic's face when he gave her the news, was critical. Hopefully it wouldn't cost her too much. Funds were getting low.

She put that depressing thought aside. Then took another look at what she was doing, trying to work up the enthusiasm that had been in short supply the last few months.

"Inspiration exists, but it has to find you working."

The quote from Pablo Picasso slid into her tired brain and she pulled a face.

Alistair brought that quote out so often she could probably say it backwards.

And right now, thoughts of Alistair were an even worse inspiration killer.

Nothing more would happen today, she realized. So, she brought her brushes to the kitchen to wash them off. She needed to get away from the project.

Cool off in this heat.

She brought the brushes back to her studio and dropped them into the jar, taking another critical look at the canvas. It wasn't coming together as she had envisioned.

Maybe she should take an artistic break from her project. Try painting something else.

Like horses, mountains, and blue skies?

Finn's comment shifted into her mind and, despite her initial annoyance with him, she had to smile.

Then she remembered what else he had told her about storing her paintings. He was probably right. She had put them in the basement because she hadn't been satisfied with them. She needed them out of her sight so she could paint without the constant judgment of her work staring at her.

But just to be safe, she brought the pieces up and set them in her studio and closed the door.

And now she needed to get outside and give herself some mental space.

Grabbing her purse, she slung it over her neck. *City habits,* she thought as she headed out the door.

Though she was on a quiet road and the only people who had come to the house were Wyatt Sutton, Reuben, and now Finn, she still felt better taking her purse and locking the door.

The sun beat down on her as she set out, and she took off the loose shirt she used as a smock and hung it over the railing leading to the house. The driveway was long, winding through trees, and as she walked, a faint breeze teased her, brushing her arms, cooling her off.

She pulled in a deep breath and let the tension that seemed to be her constant companion the past six months not exactly ease away, but at least back off for a bit.

The road was quiet, something she still had to get used to coming from downtown Vancouver where vehicles filled the roads all hours of the day and it was never silent.

Here, the lack of noise almost hurt her ears it was so complete.

After her disastrous breakup with Alistair, her counselor had recommended some time away from the city. Thankfully a friend of a friend of her sister knew of a place for rent, tucked away in the ranch land of Southern Alberta. Etta had been reluctant, seeing it as running away, but when Alistair showed up twice at her home uninvited, she finally agreed.

And now she lived on the very raggedy edge of civilization, trying to find her balance again.

A bird sent out a trilling song, a breeze soughed through the trees lining the gravel road.

As she walked, she let the peace wash over her, soothe the tension that had gripped her for the last half year. In with the good. She pulled in a long breath. Out with the bad. Slowly exhaled. Repeat.

And just when she thought she reached that lovely moment of relaxation, her phone rang.

It was her sister.

"Feeling all inspired?" was Annie's immediate question when she answered.

"Feeling peaceful," Etta said. "It's quiet here."

"Quiet is good. How's the painting going?"

Etta made a face. "Not sure if it's going or coming. I can't seem to catch any inspiration."

"Not even out there?"

Etta looked up at the blue sky with its wisps of clouds, the trees that edged the road, and shook her head. "Not really. Though I met some cowboy who thought I should paint trees, horses, and mountains. Oh, and flowers."

"Was he cute?"

Trust her sister to bring the conversation down to that level. "Yeah, he's cute. Handsome, maybe even hunky. But not for me. You know that."

"It's been eight months since him—"

"And I'm still dealing...with...him." She couldn't keep the snappy tone out of her voice.

"Is this cowboy single?" Annie pressed.

"How's the new job?" Etta needed to get her sister on another track. Even when she and Alistair were dating, Annie had been trying to get Etta to break up with him and find someone else. And for the last part of their relationship, she'd pushed even harder as Etta's own second thoughts grew.

If only she'd given Annie and her doubts more weight.

"Job is good," Annie said, "Love my boss. She gives me lots of autonomy." Annie worked as a graphic designer. She was quiet a moment, and Etta braced herself for what she sensed would come next.

"And how are you doing?" Annie asked. "Emotionally? Spiritually?"

And there they were. The deeper, darker questions.

Etta shifted her phone to her other hand, sorting through her emotions, trying to gauge what to say and how to say it. Their mother was a single parent and, while she had done her best, Annie had always been the one Eli and Etta counted on to help them through the harder parts of their lives. When she died in a single-vehicle accident, Annie, Etta, and Eli pulled together during that grueling time.

Then Etta's twin, Eli, disappeared. He'd been kayaking in Malaysia. No body was found.

Etta fell into a dark, hard place.

Six months after Eli's disappearance, Etta met Alistair. Looking back, she knew her grief and uncertainty over Eli made her more susceptible to Alistair's advances.

And advance Alistair did.

He was a respected and revered art teacher, and when she walked into that first class full of anticipation, he didn't hide his attraction or his interest. He told her she was special. Had a unique talent. He nurtured her and pursued her.

And in her weakened and vulnerable state, she soaked it up, held it all close, and gave in to her feelings for him.

But he was her professor and she was his student so they had to be careful, he kept telling her. They had to stay under the radar.

She graduated, became his TA, and still they kept things secret. She started pushing him, asking him when they could start dating in public.

He put her off and put her off and then she found out the truth about the man she'd so carelessly given her heart to.

He was married. He and his wife had two children.

And Etta still hadn't forgiven herself.

"I'm okay." She didn't want to discuss the heaviness that had dropped on her the past few days. She was tired of being a victim of her emotions.

"Are you? If you need to talk—"

"I'm not ready yet," Etta finally said, setting up the boundaries her counselor had recommended. She had spent hours and days talking with Annie and, while it helped, she knew to get past this she had to create spaces where they didn't talk about Alistair all the time.

"Okay, but you know I'm here when you are. It wasn't your fault."

Her words were supposed to be comforting but they still jarred.

"I suppose," was all Etta could give her.

"I'm right, you know. Always am. And in the meantime, you take care and give that cute cowboy a chance."

"You assume he's interested," Etta returned.

"Why wouldn't he be? You're beautiful, talented, and amazing."

And an adulteress.

The accusing words splintered her thoughts and she clenched her fists, as if ready to defend herself.

I didn't know.

"Thanks for the pep talk. But I'm saying good-bye. The cell service here is spotty and we might get cut off."

"Love you, Etta Amazing Grace."

"Love you, Annie Bo Bannie."

Etta ended the call and dropped her phone in her pocket. As she walked her mind shifted from Annie to Eli then circled around as it often did to Alistair. Thoughts of him clenched her fists and twisted her heart.

When she found out and confronted him, he assured her he and his wife had separated a year after he and Etta started dating. Which made Etta wonder if their relationship had contributed to that.

The sound of a vehicle approaching pulled her back into the present and she looked up to see a pickup truck bearing down on her, a cloud of dust swirling up behind it. Finn's truck. He slowed as he approached her, and when he came to a stop by her, his window slid down and he was smiling at her. His cowboy hat was tilted back on his head, his brown eyes crinkled up, and his teeth were white against his sun-darkened face.

Despite her protestations to her sister, her heart kicked up a notch, unconsciously acknowledging his incredible good looks and appeal.

"You're wandering far field," Finn said. "You get lost, or are you on a one-way trip looking for inspiration?" He gave a pointed look at her purse. "Or headed to town for some shopping."

She ignored his comment on her purse and looked around, trying to get her bearings. Though she had gone for walks down the road before, this was the farthest she had gone.

"I just needed to get out."

"Can't blame you. Gorgeous day. I would have a hard time being cooped up in a house slapping paint on canvas."

She tried not to bristle at his careless dismissal of her art. As if she were a house painter instead of an artist.

"Maybe I just needed to see more of those blue skies you're so enamored of."

Finn chuckled. "And horses and mountains and flowers," he added. "Don't forget about those."

"How could I?"

This elicited another chuckle. "In case you're wondering if I'm stalking you, I'm not. I'm headed to your house. The HVAC guy should be there already. Did you see him go past?"

Etta shook her head. "You're the first person I've seen since I headed out."

Finn drummed his fingers on the frame of the truck door, looking annoyed. "Hopefully he's right behind me," he said. "Are you walking all the way back to the house or do you want a ride?"

Etta had to think about that a moment. She wasn't sure she wanted to be in such close quarters with a man who appealed to her more than she cared to admit. She wasn't going down that road again. But the road she had physically gone down was long and her feet ached.

"It's a four-mile return trip if that's what you're thinking about," Finn said, appearing to read her mind.

"Then I better accept your offer," she said. She walked around the back of the truck, surprised to see Finn already at the door, holding it open.

"You move fast," Etta said.

"Not the first time I've been accused of that," he said with a flirty grin.

Despite her determination not to fall for his charms, his quick wit made her smile.

"But in this case, I'm just trying to be polite like my dear old mama taught me," he added.

"At least you can be taught," she returned as she got in.

"That's the theory." He closed the door, walked around the truck, and climbed in. He turned the radio down but hummed along to the music, tapping his fingers. "I hope country music is okay with you," he said, shooting her a quick glance.

"Your truck, your tunes," she returned.

"Do you listen to country music?"

"Not really."

"Too bad. You're missing out."

Etta listened to the nasally twang of the singer and shrugged. "Am I?"

Finn laughed. "Oh, yes. Katrina always says that country music is three chords and the truth. Lots of wisdom packed into songs about drinking, trucks, and broken hearts."

She had to chuckle at his comment. "I guess I should give it another chance."

"We could try another station." He pressed a button on his

steering wheel and flicked through a few more stations then stopped. "Let's try this one. Oldies."

A classic pop song came to an end and then the music shifted and a guitar played a few soft, plaintive notes.

"This could be your theme song," Finn said, turning the sound up a little.

Etta frowned, listening to the words.

"Hello darkness, my old friend," the singer sang over the guitar's soft notes.

She listened, then shrugged. "Sorry?" was all she said.

"Darkness? Black? Your favorite color?"

She gave him a wry look. "You're so perceptive."

He flashed her a return grin. "It's a gift."

"You have just the one?"

"Okay, I have many, but I don't want to flaunt them. Makes people feel insecure."

Etta couldn't stop the unladylike snort of laughter that escaped.

In response Finn turned up the radio and began singing along, which made her chuckle. When the song was done, he shot her another grin. "You have a cute giggle."

"Thank you? I guess?"

"You sound like you're not sure what to do with that."

"I'm not, quite frankly. I've never been told I have a cute giggle."

"A first for everything. That's why it's worth getting up in the morning." Finn switched the radio station again and then again.

"What are you looking for?" she asked after he switched it yet again.

"And isn't that the existential question of the year," he said, sounding pensive. Then he grinned again. "Just station surfing. Like channel surfing, except on the radio."

Which made her smile again. Something about this guy

made her chuckle. His confidence and humor were refreshing.

And he was cute.

Etta immediately dismissed that. To center herself, she pulled her focus back to the painting she was struggling with. Maybe she should start over. The thought made her inwardly groan. She'd already done two of the four panels. Could she really paint over them?

"So, not liking my musical chairs?"

"Pardon me?"

"The constantly switching music. It's making you look thoughtful."

"Rats. I was going for pensive," she quipped back.

He laughed at her response, then grinned at her. "Mission accomplished. So, what turned your smile upside down?"

"Just...stuff," she said, waving off his concern.

"Like how you'll work a horse into your next painting?" He gave her a sly grin. "I know you want to."

This elicited another laugh. Seriously, this guy could get any girl he wanted with an attitude like he had.

"You never know which beasts lurk in the background of my paintings," she said.

"How did you get started with painting? I've never met a painter before, so I'm curious."

His comment made her grin, and she resisted the urge to make some quip about painters working on large canvases like houses and walls. "I've always loved creating art. Started with finger painting and graduated to the brush."

"You go to school for that? Katrina said something about you working for a university before you came here."

And just like that, Alistair was back. She brushed his memory from her mind, focusing on the road ahead. She didn't realize she had walked this far and was glad she had accepted the ride from Finn.

"I did. I'm taking a sabbatical to build up my portfolio. I've applied for a position as an artist-in-residence that I hope to hear back from."

Finn acknowledged that with a slow nod, as if absorbing this. "Okay. I guess that means something to somebody."

"It means if I get that job, I'll have a shot at a tenured position at the university. In other words, a job for the rest of my life."

"Sounds a lot like ranching," he joked.

She smiled again, but then as they turned down the driveway, she sat up, frowning.

"Is that smoke?" Finn asked a split second before she was about to.

He stepped on the gas and swerved around the last corner just in time to see smoke billowing out of the basement window.

"My paintings," Etta cried out as Finn slammed on the brakes, turned off the truck, and jumped out. She was seconds behind him.

Panic clawed at her at the thought of all that work going up in flames. She might get them.

"Etta, stop," Finn called out.

"I have to rescue my paintings." Heart slamming in her chest, she ran on shaky legs up the ramp and was about to yank open the door when Finn scooped his arm around her waist and pulled her back.

"No. Don't open that door," he growled, dragging her back down the ramp.

"I have to go inside." She tried to fight him, but his arm was like a band of steel, solid and immovable.

"You don't know what will happen when you do," Finn said, his voice loud in her ear. She heard the edge of panic, which only increased hers.

"But I can't let them burn. They're just inside the porch." Another futile attempt to push his arm away.

"Doesn't matter," he said, pulling her farther from the house. "If you open that door, you'll let a lot of oxygen get into the house and you could end up creating a massive fireball."

She tried one more time to fight him off, but it was futile. Then, as she watched, the windows of the basement cracked, blew in, and a ball of flame burst out.

She could have been in there, she realized, sagging against Finn, terror washing over her.

Still holding her, Finn pulled out his phone, dialing one-handed as he led her farther away. "Got a fire," he said, giving the department the address.

Etta wondered why he even bothered. Town was half an hour away. How long would it take the fire trucks to arrive? What good could they do?

Another window popped, another roar, and now flames licked up the side of the house.

Everything she owned was inside. But that mattered little compared to all her paintings.

Her entry to a new and better stage of her life.

Disappearing before her eyes.

CHAPTER TWO

Still holding Etta, Finn dialed Reuben's number. He answered on the first ring, sounding put out.

"Your old house is on fire. Thought I'd let you know," was all he managed.

"What? Is Etta inside?"

"No. She was on a walk when it started."

He looked down at Etta, who now clung to his arm, her fingers digging in. At least she wasn't fighting him anymore. "I'll call the neighbors and be right there," Reuben said.

Finn put his phone away. He doubted the fire trucks would come soon enough. Doubted Reuben and whoever he could wrangle to come could do anything.

The fire roared now, flames darting in and out of the basement windows. He felt the heat growing, coming off the house.

"We need to move away," he said to Etta, who was fixated on the house, anguish twisting her features.

"No. We need to put the fire out. Don't you have a hose? Some garden hose or something."

"It's on the house, Etta. It won't work." He moved away from the house, still holding her in case she felt the need to rescue her work.

"But surely there's something we can do," she said, looking back as he led her to a safer distance.

"Sorry, we just have to wait."

"But the trucks won't come in time." She gave one last feeble attempt to pull away, as if she was ready to tackle the fire herself. "All my work. All my canvases," she choked out.

He wished he could say something to encourage her, but knew it was pointless.

So he just kept holding her, supporting her while the fire grew.

And then, just like that, the fight left her. She sagged back against him and then turned, burying her face against him, as if she couldn't watch. His heart ached for her. Sure, it sucked to see the house burn down, but for her it was all her belongings. All the work she had done on her paintings.

With a sigh, he slipped his other arm around her, holding her close, giving her what slight comfort he could.

She didn't cry, just stayed where she was, her hands clutching her head.

Despite all the drama surrounding them, it felt good to have her in his arms. She was tall, but she fit just right, her head tucked under his chin.

Finn quashed that thought. How could he contemplate that right now?

"I'm so sorry," was all he could say as she stayed curled against him.

Then she drew in a long, slow breath and pulled away. Her eyes shone with unshed tears, but her chin came up, her head held high.

Spunky. He liked that.

"So we just wait?" she managed.

"Yeah." He wasn't sure if he should keep holding her. But then she stepped away from him, so that was that.

She turned to face the fire, as if challenging it to break her.

"I'm so sorry about your stuff."

"It's just stuff," she said, her voice holding a note of anguish. He wanted to hug her again but knew that would be inappropriate.

Heat poured off the fire. They moved farther away. Finn was worried about the furnace and the gas lines, not sure what would happen as the flames grew, taking over more of the house.

A truck roared into the yard, followed by another one.

Reuben jumped out of the vehicle and came to stand beside Finn and Etta. "Did you get anything out?" he asked.

"No. We got here too late. Sorry, man."

Reuben shoved his hands into his pockets, staring at the house, shaking his head as the roar grew louder. "I'm sorry too." He heaved out a sigh, shaking his head in disbelief.

"Isn't there anything you can do?" Etta asked, turning to him.

"I wish we could," Reuben said. "Looks like it's too big now for us to do anything. If we could have caught it sooner..." He let the sentence trail off.

"I was gone when it started. I'm so sorry," Etta said.

"It's not your fault."

"Something was wrong with the furnace," she said, her tone plaintive. "I should have been more careful."

"Stop," Finn said, laying an assuring hand on her shoulder. "We don't know what happened."

A few, long, agony-filled minutes later, the fire trucks pulled up. And there was nothing to do but watch.

"So, it's not much, but it should work out for now," Finn said, standing in the middle of the cabin on the ranch, looking around, trying to see it through Etta's eyes. It looked cozy to him. He'd always loved staying here when he was younger. It wasn't huge. It had a small bedroom, a dining area with a leather couch and chair, and kitchen cabinets tucked in the corner with a small stove and refrigerator.

It could work for a while.

Etta sat on the couch, looking exhausted, and he didn't blame her. She had just seen most of her earthly possessions and her artwork go up in flames not four hours ago. The firemen got the fire under control and the structure was salvaged, but everything inside it was smoke damaged, scorched, or burnt. They couldn't go inside until the fire inspector came.

"Carly said she was coming by with some clothes for you," Finn said. "I hope you don't mind, but she guessed that she was about your size. Maybe shorter."

Etta nodded, her hands resting on her knees as she looked around. "Thanks for this," she said, her voice quiet. "I appreciate you and your family doing this for me."

"Of course," Finn said. "The house you were renting belongs to us. We gotta give you a place to stay."

She looked over at him and the lost look on her face cut him to the core. "This feels surreal yet."

"I'm sure it does." He wanted to comfort her like he had at the house. But that might seem like he was taking advantage.

"So, what's next?" she asked.

"I'm not sure," he said, rubbing his temple with his forefinger, trying to think. "Once the fire inspector is done, the insurance company takes over. Reuben is talking to them now. He'll let you know what happens next. I'm sure they'll want a list of everything you had in the house."

Etta's lips puffed out a sigh. "I can't even think about that right now."

"Then don't." He hesitated, not sure what to say or do next. "I'm sorry you had to deal with all of this," was all he could say.

She nodded, but he caught the shimmer of tears in her eyes as she sucked in a shuddering breath.

Enough with trying to be all chivalrous. The sight of her breaking down was too much for him to handle. He sat down beside her, let her know he was there to help. He was just trying to show support, but when she lowered her head, pressing the heels of her hands to her eyes, he had to do something.

He put his arm around her. To his surprise, once again, she leaned in. It should have felt awkward but it wasn't. It felt pretty good, actually, at least on his side of things.

"It will work out," he said to her, rubbing his hand on her arm. "It will all work out." Lame and maybe a bit slick, but it was all he could offer her right now.

Her narrow shoulders shuddered and he guessed she was trying to hold her grief back. He could only imagine how difficult this was for her. She was in a strange place. She had just lost all her work. He had no idea how long it took her to do a painting, but she had a number of them stacked in the basement.

Probably all toast now.

All she had was the clothes on her back, her purse, and her cell phone lying beside her on the couch.

She was the first to pull away, and he felt a sense of loss when she did. He kind of enjoyed being a comforter to her.

He reined in his thoughts and reactions and moved away, standing up to give her some space.

"I'm sorry," she muttered, looking away, her cheeks pink. "It's been that kind of day."

A knock on the door stopped anything else he might say.

"Come in," Etta managed. Finn stepped away from the couch, thankful they weren't sitting together anymore. That would have been awkward.

Carly pushed open the door, and poked her head inside.

"Hey, thought I would drop some clothes off for you. Some are mine but I stuck my neck out and went to town to get some, well, personal items."

Carly shot Finn a warning glance, but there was no way he was following up on that.

This was his cue to leave. "I'm heading out now." He turned to Etta. "If you need anything, just text me. I think Reuben will know a bit more about the house once he talks to the adjuster."

Etta gave him a vague smile as she stood, running her hands down her paint-smeared pants.

He wanted to say something to reassure her but guessed anything he wanted to say would be superficial and unwelcome.

So he left, closing the door behind him.

But as he walked away from the cabin, he thought of the moments he and Etta had shared and the surprising feeling of connection they created.

CHAPTER THREE

*E*tta walked up the steps of the main house, glancing around, feeling like she was trespassing.

The yard was a busy place if yesterday was anything to go by. After Carly dropped the very welcome clothing items off yesterday, including brand new undergarments still in the package and a few toiletries, Adele had stopped by the cabin and invited her to join them for dinner, saying that she understood if she didn't want to. Etta thanked her and turned down the offer, saying she wasn't really hungry.

Nor was she in the mood to sit with so many unfamiliar people.

But half an hour later Katrina came to the house with a plate of food for her and pointed out the small microwave on the counter to heat it up with, telling her she would also bring some more flowers for the cabin. Later, Etta needed to get out. So she went for a walk, giving herself some time to pray and wonder what her next step should be.

She had tried to call Annie but there was no reply. She didn't feel like leaving a message. On her way back she heard children laughing, then someone calling them. She knew that Wyatt, the owner of the ranch with Reuben and Finn, had three children. A young boy, aged six, and twin girls, age three.

By the time she got back in the yard, the kids were already in the house.

Then, this morning, Reuben gave her some groceries Adele and Carly had put together for her and an update from the insurance adjuster. She was coming today, and Wyatt would meet her at the house when she did.

But now Etta needed something even more important than food and clothes. Even more important than her now burnt-up art supplies. She knocked on the door.

The door opened and Carly stood there, smiling at her.

"Come on in," she said, gesturing to her as she stepped aside. "You don't need to knock. Just walk in the house."

Etta knew that wasn't happening, but she smiled.

"Hey, nice shirt," Carly said, grinning.

Etta glanced down at the yellow-and-white-striped button-down. "Thanks, and I appreciate you giving it to me."

"Looks better on you than me," Carly said with a sigh. "Your red hair makes it look amazing. Of course, your red hair is amazing, period."

Etta wasn't sure how to respond to the compliment.

"But I'm guessing you didn't come to talk about fashion choices," Carly continued. "Come on in."

Etta hesitated then stepped inside.

"Do you want some tea?" Carly asked as she led the way through the large porch with its double benches. Coats were strung up on hooks, boots and shoes of all sizes were tucked in cubbies or scattered on the floor. It looked like the busy home Etta knew it could be.

"I'm fine, thanks."

"Did you have breakfast? Do you need something to eat?"

"No. Thanks. I'm not very hungry."

"Stress can be a real appetite killer. Did you sleep okay?"

"Not really." It had been hard to dismiss the memories of the smell of the smoke, the sound of the flames and, even worse, the panic that twisted through her as she watched all her hard work destroyed.

She had been behind before this. Now?

"I can imagine. Sit down."

Etta hesitated. She didn't want to take up Carly's time so came directly to the reason she had come here.

"I was wondering if you had a Bible," she said, still standing.

Carly frowned, as if considering this request, and Etta wondered if she had overstepped some invisible boundary.

"Unless it's a problem," she said. She knew the Suttons went to church. But maybe they didn't read the Bible at home?

"No. Not a problem at all," Carly assured her, waving off her question. "There's more than enough Bibles in this house."

Her voice held a curious edge. Defensive, it seemed to Etta.

"Follow me," Carly continued. "I'm sure we can find one somewhere."

The doors of the kitchen/dining room opened and three kids burst into the room.

They skidded to a halt when they saw Etta.

"Hi, you," one of the twin girls said.

"Hi, yourself," Etta said, smiling at the sight of the twins. They wore pink T-shirts with sparkly hearts and pink leggings. They both wore high ponytails clipped into place with bright pink bows. Two little bubblegum beauties. A young boy hung back, looking at her curiously.

"I am Maya. This is Maria, and that boy is Dean," the one girl said, pointing to the young boy. "And I think you are Etta."

"That's what Dad told us," Dean said. "She's staying with us because her house burned down."

Maya looked intrigued. "Like a fire? Like with flames and smoke and everything?"

Her questions brought the memory of yesterday crashing into Etta's already weary mind. All she could do was nod.

"Did you get burnt?" Maria asked.

"Okay, you three, why are you hanging around here?" An older woman followed them into the room, her gray hair pulled back in a half ponytail. She wore a plaid shirt over a tank top and blue jeans. Etta wondered if she was the kid's grandmother. "You're supposed to be getting your boots on to go outside."

Then she saw Etta and her grin shifted to a sympathetic smile.

"Hi, I'm Ruby Mulder," she said, her hand resting on the little boy's shoulder. "I try to take care of these little hooligans while Wyatt and Adele are working." So, not the grandmother.

Etta nodded at her. "Nice to meet you."

"Is it nice to meet us?" Maya put her hands on her hips, her head cocked to one side.

Etta had to chuckle at her question. "Yes, it's nice to meet you as well," she said.

"We're not hooligans," Maria said. "Miss Ruby just calls us that for fun."

"Aren't you?" Ruby asked with a gentle chuckle. "Because I think you are."

Maria shook her head as if to negate that comment. "Our daddy and our mommy say we're good kids."

"Then prove your daddy and mommy right and head outside," Ruby said.

"I want to talk to you, but we need lots of fresh air." Maya addressed her comment to Etta. "My daddy says it makes us tired, and that makes him happy. Do you like fresh air? Uncle Finn said you go on long walks."

That Finn was talking about her made her blush a little. "I like walking."

"It's good for the soul," Ruby said. "Especially out here in the country. Finn also said that you're an artist. That you paint. I'm sure you'll find lots of inspiration out here."

Mountains and flowers, Etta thought, a fresh pain lancing through her at the thought of all her art supplies now lost to her as well.

"I hope to, once I can get painting again."

"Are you having supper with us tonight?" Maria asked.

"I don't think so," Etta said, though the look of disappointment on the little girl's face almost made her change her mind.

"You should. You could help me draw some pretty pictures," Maria said. "I like drawing."

"Don't make Miss Etta feel guilty," Ruby said. "I'm sure she could use the time alone."

She'd had a surfeit of time alone the past few weeks. Though it had been the reason she'd come out here, being in this house only the few moments she'd had made her realize how much she'd missed human company.

"And all her stuff burnt in the fire," the little boy said. "So she probably doesn't have anything to help you."

"But she could still teach me," Maria said.

"Enough pestering. We need to get going." Ruby turned to Etta. "I'm sure I'll see you out and about now that you're here. And you take care, honey. I'm sorry to hear about what you had to deal with. But you're in excellent hands with the Sutton family. They'll take care of you."

Etta's throat thickened at the woman's sympathy. *Kindness of strangers,* she thought.

As the door closed behind Ruby and the kids, Carly came into the kitchen, holding a stack of books.

"Sorry to keep you waiting. I would have been here sooner, but I got a call from my contractor I had to take, the irresponsible louse." She blew out a sigh and shook her head. "Anyhow, not your concern, but I found some options for you." She set three Bibles on the table. "You can pick which one you want."

"Are you sure I am not taking anyone's away?" Did this family really have three extra Bibles?

"Trust me, no. There's a few more scattered around the house somewhere and a couple here in the dining room. We are a Bible-believing family. For the most part."

Did she imagine the faintly sarcastic tone in her voice?

Etta pushed her reaction down, trying to choose one of the Bibles. Last night she had been stressed, grieving, and confused and had missed the comfort her Bible could have given her and the outlet her painting would have. She was thankful that she could at least have a Bible. Her art supplies would have to come later.

"I see my clothes for you aren't too bad," Carly said. "Pants are a little short, though."

"I'm hoping to go clothes shopping tomorrow, so I'll be okay."

"Finn said your car was at the mechanic, so do you want me to take you shopping?"

Etta hesitated, not sure what she should do.

"I know all the stores in town," Carly said. "And Finn also said something about your paints and art supplies. I'm sure you'll want to replace those."

Again, that clutch of uncertainty blended with anxiety. How was she supposed to replace all the paintings she had lost and create enough for the gallery showing? Especially feeling the way she did right now, lost, bereft, and stressed. "Apparently, I have to wait to see what the insurance adjuster says before I dare buy more."

"Is there a place in Calgary you could order from?"

"Actually, there's a couple," Etta said. "I've ordered from one of them before."

"I need to make a trip into Calgary tomorrow to check out some stuff for the event center. I could take you."

"Okay. That could work," Etta said. She needed to get going right away, but until her car was fixed, she would have to depend on other people's generosity.

"Good. It'll be nice to have company on the drive." Carly waved her hand over the books. "So, take your pick. I can guarantee you none of them will be missed."

Etta chose the one nearest to her, picked it up, and held it close. As if drawing some comfort from it.

"Thanks again for all your help."

Carly's phone rang, and she pulled it out and made a face. "It's my contractor again," she muttered. "Sorry. I have to take this."

Etta took this as her cue, waggled a good-bye, then left.

She stepped out, taking a moment to appreciate the sunshine, drawing in a long slow breath, struggling to stifle the ever-present panic bubbling just below the surface.

All shall be well, and all shall be well and all manner of things shall be well.

The quote from Julian of Norwich settled her swirling thoughts. She took another calming breath then walked down the stairs, clutching her Bible, headed for the cabin.

"Hey, Etta, wait up."

Finn's voice resounded across the yard and produced a most unwelcome slip in her heart. Etta swallowed against her reaction then stopped, turning as Finn jogged over toward her. He pushed his hat back on his head and grinned at her. "How are you doing? Really doing?" His sincerity flowed out of his voice.

"Still a little shaky," she admitted.

Finn held her gaze, his expression growing serious. "I'm surprised you're only shaky," he said. "That was truly terrifying. I'm just glad you weren't in the house when it happened."

She was as well.

"I should let you know Wyatt is at the house with the adjuster," Finn continued. "He said he'd let you know anything he learns."

"Thanks."

Finn angled his chin toward the book she carried. "Some reading material?"

Etta looked down at it, her fingers curling around its spine. "It's a Bible I got from Carly. I hope that's okay."

"Of course it is. Thanks to my mom, there are Bibles all over the house." Finn chuckled. "I think she collected them. Gave one to each of us and had a few to spare. I know for a fact Carly isn't reading any of them."

Etta wondered at his comment but decided not to follow up on it.

"As for the rest of your stuff, I'm sure you're anxious to know what you can replace once the adjuster does her thing."

"I don't know if I can wait for that," Etta said, the all-too familiar thread of panic tightening around her stomach. "I need to get working. I was behind already. Now—" to her dismay, her throat choked off anything else she had to say.

Finn's expression grew troubled. "Now you're way behind. How many paintings did you have done for your resident artist thing?"

Despite the panic curling in her midsection at all that rode on those paintings, she had to smile at his attempt at naming her position. "Five. I was working on number six."

"You look worried, and I don't blame you. All that work you might have lost, will you be able to make it up?"

"I don't have any choice. I have to start over." And where would that inspiration come from now?

"And you'll need to get paints and brushes and stuff."

"I do. Thankfully, Carly said she has to go to Calgary tomorrow. So, she can take me to an art supply store I found."

"I know. I have to pick up some filters for the tractor they didn't have in stock in town so I'm going with her too. She said she needed moral support. Things haven't been going great for her with her event center."

Second thoughts chased through Etta's brain. She wasn't sure spending a day with Finn was such a good idea. He was too appealing, and she couldn't allow herself even the tiniest shift from her purpose. But if Carly came that would change the dynamic.

"I'm not sure I want to shop with you breathing down my neck," she joked, taking refuge in humor. "My brother Eli used to—" She clamped her lips together, catching herself, her heart stuttering. Why had that memory jolted into her mind?

Finn shook his head, apparently missing her slip. "I'm a good shopper. I'm patient, and as long as I have a fully charged phone, I'm good. Besides, might be interesting to see what kind of paint you get."

"You make it sound like I'm going to the hardware store to pick up whitewash," Etta returned.

Finn smiled at her. "Nice to see the spunk hasn't left you."

Why did that comment make her blush?

"Just come," he said. "If you're under the gun, like you seem to be saying, you'll want to get working as soon as possible. Besides, you'll need something to distract you after what you've been through."

Etta wasn't sure a trip to Calgary would serve as the distraction Finn thought it would, but he was right about one thing. She needed to get to work as soon as possible and in order for that to happen, she would need supplies.

"Okay. I think I'll take you up on it."

It was the logical thing to do. But when he grinned at her, his hands strung up in his pockets, his hat pulled back on his head, framing his too-handsome face, she couldn't stop the feeling that she was making a mistake.

CHAPTER FOUR

inn knocked on Etta's door, hoping she'd gotten the text he sent her last night about their departure time. It was a two-hour drive to Calgary, and he wanted to get an early start.

But she opened it immediately and gave him a vague smile. She wore blue jeans and a white shirt. Simple but classy. Sure, they were probably Carly's clothes, but she wore them well. "Just give me a minute to get my purse," she said.

Finn tried not to snoop, but he couldn't help but look into the cabin as she walked to the bedroom. He and Carly had cleaned it up as best as they could. He hoped it was okay with her. Of course, she had nothing to add to the decor. All her stuff was still at the house. What hadn't been scorched or burnt.

She came walking out, her hair pulled back in a ponytail, her purse slung over her shoulder. As she closed the door, she hesitated. "I noticed the lock on the door doesn't work," she said.

"No. We don't lock our doors out here."

"Oh. I see." She bit her lip.

"If that's a concern, we can stop at the hardware store in Millars Crossing on our way back from Calgary."

"I don't want to put you out."

"And I don't want you to stress about someone breaking into your cabin, though bears are a bigger concern. Bears and the kids." He lifted his hands in a what-can-you-do gesture. "Not sure which is worse."

She laughed at that, which made Finn feel even better about himself. Always good when a pretty woman laughs at your feeble jokes.

"We'll take my truck," Finn said as he stood aside for her to go ahead of him. "I hope that's okay with you."

"I'm just along for the ride. It's like the old saying, beggars can't be choosers. I don't mind riding in the truck."

"So, you have the address of where we need to go for you?" he asked as they walked along. Frogs were croaking in the pond and the trill of blackbirds sounded through the air. Summer was here, and life was good. For the first time in a long time, he felt a sense of peace.

"I have a couple of options," she said, holding her purse close to herself.

"We can go to both."

"Maybe, but one is right downtown. I didn't think you'd want to go there, especially now that we're taking your truck."

"Hey girl, I've driven this thing through enough Tim Horton drive-throughs, I can maneuver downtown Calgary. So, if you change your mind, that's fine with me." Finn grinned.

Etta's returning smile created that same loopy curl of attraction.

"Well, that's good to know if I need to go there."

They got to the truck and Etta paused, looking around. "Where's Carly?"

Finn pulled his keys out of his front pocket, shrugging. "She should be coming any minute. She's usually punctual."

Etta checked her purse to make sure she had her phone, thankful, once again, that she'd been paranoid about leaving her purse in the house before the fire. At least she had her phone, identification and, more important, her credit card.

She looked around as they waited, feeling a twinge of regret. It was a beautiful sunny day. Almost too nice to spend the day in a vehicle or shopping. But before the fire she had spent day after day cooped up in the house. Pushing herself, trying to get work done. This outing would be good for her.

"That girl better show up soon." Finn sounded irritated.

Then the door of the house opened and Carly strode down the steps and toward them, a look of extreme frustration on her face. "I can't come with you guys," she said, sounding irritated, waving her arms to underline her mood. "I just got a call from the contractor. He wants me to meet with him. I'm afraid it won't be good news."

"You don't know that for sure," Finn said.

"Anytime I've talked to him the past week, it's not been good news," Carly snapped. "I doubt this will be any different. But that means I can't go to Calgary with you. Which really annoys me. I've got a ton of work to do and don't have time for this prima donna. I wish I could fire him."

"Then do."

Carly heaved out another sigh, shaking her head. "I'm too far into the project now to find anyone else. Anyhow, you two have fun. I'll have to go on my own some other time."

You two.

Etta wasn't sure she liked the sound of that. Spending an entire day with only Finn wasn't the plan. She was okay with being with him as long as Carly was along. But now?

However, it would look awkward and foolish if she backed out now. Besides, the clock and calendar were working against her. The sooner she got her supplies, the sooner she could get back to work.

"I'm sorry about this," Carly said to Etta. "But you're in good hands with Finn instead of me."

"You driving us to Calgary was never an option," Finn said. "I refuse to put my life in your hands."

"What? I'm a good driver."

"Four speeding tickets in the past year. And two parking tickets."

"Parking tickets have nothing to do with my driving ability," Carly retorted.

"And she conveniently ignores the speeding tickets," Finn said with a shrug and a look heavenward.

"I don't have the mental energy to wrangle with you," Carly said. "But we'll finish this discussion another time. I can't let you put down my driving ability and just walk away."

Finn chuckled and turned to Etta. "Well I guess we better get going then while I'm still ahead." He opened the door for her and gestured for her to step inside.

"Oh, look at you," Carly teased. "All gentlemanly and such."

Finn put his finger to his lips. "Be quiet, my dear," he said to his sister. "I'm trying desperately to make a good impression."

"Just don't be too desperate," Carly said. "Girls can smell that a mile away."

Despite her concern, Etta grinned as she climbed into the truck and buckled her seat belt. She got along well with her sister, but they never teased each other like Finn and his family did.

Finn got in the truck and started it up and a few minutes later they headed down the road. Too late for second thoughts. So Etta settled into the leather seats, determined to enjoy the ride.

"So, what made you get into being an artist?" Finn asked once they were on the road. He had turned his radio off, and Etta welcomed the silence. Her head was tired from all the thinking she'd been doing the past day.

"I always liked drawing and painting. I used to get into trouble at school for always doodling in the margins of my workbooks. Though Mrs. Abernathy, my third-grade teacher, didn't mind. In fact, she was the one who encouraged my mom to enroll me in art classes."

"You must have loved that," Finn said.

"I would have, but we couldn't afford it."

"That's too bad. Did you have a big family?"

"No. Just small paychecks. There were only four of us. My mom, me, Annie and...and Eli."

And just like that, the mere mention of her brother's name resurrected a dull ache, the usual choking sensation. She turned away, struggling to breathe, struggling to release emotions that clogged her throat.

Thankfully, Finn said nothing. Instead, he turned the radio on to country music. He kept it quiet, humming along as he drove. He could carry a tune spot-on, she thought as she pulled herself back on track.

"Do Annie and Eli live close to you?" he asked after a while.

His question was a casual one. The kind people ask as they're getting to know each other.

Normally she would be able to relay the information. But somehow trying to explain to Finn, a man who had already comforted her once as she watched her work being destroyed, made her throat thicken. She blamed her lapse on the fragility of her emotions the past few days.

The past few months, if she was honest.

She had always thought of herself as strong, but Alistair and his lies had stolen much of her confidence and balance.

"Annie lives in Vancouver," she finally said. "And my brother..." Again, her voice faltered as her throat thickened. Once again, she felt as if the tears were locked in her chest, unable to come out, choking her.

"Eli, my brother... He died in Malaysia. At least we think he did." She stopped there, pursing her lips and slowly blowing out the air she had sucked in.

"What do you mean, think?"

Another breath, another swallow to ease the pressure in her throat. "The authorities never found a body. Just the empty kayak that he'd rented. It had washed up on shore with some of his things inside. We never found out exactly what happened."

She blinked, looking away, not wanting him to see the anguish that could still contort her features at the memory of her brother, dying alone.

And once again, she wished she could cry. Wished she could shed the tears Annie had. Maybe it would ease the stone of anguish lodged in her chest.

"That must have been hard. No closure for your family."

All she could manage was a tight nod.

"Was he older or younger than you?" Finn continued.

"He was my twin."

Another beat of silence, then she felt his hand on her shoulder, a gentle squeeze, nothing more.

But to her surprise, his touch comforted her. Alistair had been understanding, but his entire focus was on her work. Her paintings, telling her this was a way to express her overwhelming grief.

"My brothers aren't my twins, but I would be gutted if anything happened to them. I can't imagine what it would be like for you. Like you lost half of yourself."

"That's exactly how it feels," she said, surprised at his perception, grateful for his understanding. She'd received sympathy from other people after Eli's disappearance, but this was the first time someone understood how devastating her loss had been.

"And then not knowing what happened..." He paused, holding her gaze, then looking back at the road. "I think I would always be waiting for better news."

"We were. I kept holding on to a hope that they had made a mistake. That it wasn't his kayak. That someday he would come up the walk, his duffel bag slung over his shoulder—" Again her voice gave out.

She stopped, knowing she was talking too much. He probably wanted to be done with this subject.

"Did he travel a lot?" he asked finally.

His question surprised her. Most people, when confronted with her grief, changed the subject or said nothing at all. They seldom asked her more questions. Talking about Eli hurt, but ignoring her grief altogether cut even deeper.

"He did," she said, allowing herself to shift back to older memories of him. "He would work until he made enough money to travel, head out the door, and come back when the money ran out."

Finn angled her a crooked grin. "He sounds like I guy I would have enjoyed meeting. I did the same thing for the past few years."

"Really? You seem like such a cowboy."

"I am, but I had my moments of rebellion. Of feeling stuck in Millars Crossing. When Reuben got married, I figured..." He let the sentence drift off and Etta sensed there were other reasons he wasn't ready to talk about. "I wasn't the only Sutton who scooted out of Millars Crossing. Carly also had plans of being a permanent resident until her life went south and she needed a change. Just like me."

His vague words both about Carly and himself piqued her interest. But at the same time, she wasn't sure she was ready to bring other people's pasts into her life when she had so much of her own stuff to deal with.

So she didn't follow up on his comments.

"Which places did you go?" she asked, preferring to focus on something less personal.

"I initially hit the usual tourist hot spots. Rome, Paris, Machu Picchu. Once I got the bug though, I got more adventurous." He glanced sidelong at her. "What about Eli? Where had he gone?"

"He did a hike up the Pacific Crest Trail. That was hard. Didn't hear from him much then. He went to Belarus, Croatia, Jordan, Israel, parts of Africa and Asia. I had a hard time keeping up with all the places he went. He would send pictures and stories whenever he could. I never had a desire to travel like he did, so it was fun to travel vicariously with him."

"That's a lot of places. I never did any hiking, but I did get to Jordan and Israel as well. I loved that trip."

"Israel was one country I really wanted to visit. Just never had the time or the money. Art school took up too much of both. And after that, trying to get my masters, until—" She stopped herself, knowing she ventured to a place she wanted to avoid. "But Eli just did what he wanted. I was always a little jealous of that independence. I was more security oriented. Needed to have my ducks in a row, all fluffy and tidy."

Finn chuckled at that. "Whereas I would probably want to stir those ducks up to see them fly. Tell them to be free."

"I'm glad you never got to meet my ducks," she returned.

Another welcome hoot of laughter that lightened the atmosphere.

"So, you like security," he said.

"You make that sound like a dirty word."

"No, not at all. Just trying to feel you out. Get to know you better."

She almost asked, to what end?

Instead, she said, "Always did. Eli never understood it either."

"I think I do understand," Finn said. "I used to love adventure and uncertainty, but that changed."

"What made that happen?" She was curious now.

His ever-present cowboy hat was set back on his head, so she could see the crease of a frown on his forehead. He was quiet for a while and she wondered if he would answer her.

Then he shrugged, as if he had made up his mind. "A combination of things." Another moment of silence, then he grinned at her again. "I was in Bangkok healing up from a free soloing accident in Muaklek Cliff. Free soloing is rock climbing without a rope."

"I know what free soloing is," Etta said with a wry smile. "Eli did that in Patagonia one year." She couldn't stop a shiver of apprehension. Finn sounded more and more like her brother all the time. "I think the two of you would have gotten along well."

"Sounds like we could have traded some stories." He grew serious. "Anyhow, I was with my buddy, Rob. He was supposed to go first, but he asked if I would. I didn't care. I went up, but I knew he was coming behind me. I felt pressured, so I went too fast. Missed a handhold and fell. I broke my arm, fractured my shin, and ripped open my leg. My helmet fell off, and I missed hitting my head on a sharp rock by mere inches. It was so close. Rob had to drag me out of there. I was losing blood and floating in and out of consciousness. It was freaky. When I was conscious, I prayed. Hard. I prayed harder than I ever had. I still don't know how I got to the hospital. Rob dropped me off and flaked out on me, scared he would get charged with something, still not sure what. The doctor told me that he couldn't believe I didn't die. I said it was because I had a family who was praying for me, even though they had no clue where I was. Told me how lucky I was. I took that as a sign to quit. Head home before something did me in for real."

Despite her concern and previous unease, she smiled at his story.

"Nice to know you can be taught," she said.

"I'm thin-skinned but thick-skulled. Saved me too many times but also got me into trouble too many times. But the near-death experience showed me I was pushing my luck. Even more, I found that I missed my family and was tired of the running around. Trying to find the next thrill, the next adventure. So I came back."

"Are you settled in?"

"I hope so." He shrugged. "If I traveled again, I would be more careful."

"But you might go again?"

Another shrug. "I guess I'd need a reason to stick around."

"And the ranch isn't reason enough?"

"I love being with my brothers, but I have to admit, it's kind of hard seeing them all settled down."

"You don't have any desire to follow in their footsteps? Find someone to settle down with?"

"At one time I had plans."

He didn't say anything more, which made her even more curious. Normally she would have left it, but something about Finn made her want to delve a bit deeper.

"So, what happened?"

"My future bride dumped me. I had saved up a bunch of money for the wedding, so I used it to travel instead."

As his words registered, she felt bad for pressing. "I shouldn't have been nosy. It was none of my business. I'm sorry."

"Don't be. I don't mind talking about it. But everything turned out for the best. At the time, I wasn't committed to staying on the ranch, and her career would have meant a move to the city. I discovered through my travels that I'm not cut out for city life. So not such a sad ending after all." He shot her another glance. "And that's my story. What about you? What deep nefarious secrets do you have in your past?"

Shock jolted through her. His question landed with painful precision on the waves of guilt that surged through her at times. She pushed down her reaction, reminding herself that those mistakes were in the past.

"Too many to list," she said, hoping she sounded light and airy. Like it was a joke.

"So you said you always wanted to be an artist." He switched to something else. "How did you get to where you are now?"

"I took art in high school. I had a really good teacher who helped me apply for some scholarships. That's what paid for university."

"Cool."

"Actually, in my high school, art wasn't cool at all."

"Pfft." Finn waved his hand. "I wasn't cool in high school either."

"Really? I can't imagine that. Such a good-looking cowboy." As soon as the words popped out of her mouth, she wanted to take them back.

Maybe he wouldn't notice.

But Finn pulled down the rearview mirror, angled his head this way and that, made a face, then pushed it back up, shaking his head. "Not seeing it, darlin'," he said with a Texas twang.

She chuckled at his antics, thankful he had turned it into a joke.

"So what do you learn in school that you can't learn on your own?" he continued.

"Different techniques. You study how the classical painters worked to learn from them. Each prof had their own area of expertise."

"And did one of those profs teach you how to do what you do now?"

His question was simple. Just curiosity, but it created a

thrum of anxiety that was immediately followed by anger that Alistair could still have this hold over her emotions.

"I was guided, yes. Told what my strengths were." She kept it short and simple. "What about you? No desire to go further in school?"

"Are you kidding? Me and school were mortal enemies. I barely scraped through high school. Couldn't wait to be done so I could figure out what else I didn't want to do."

She chuckled at that, and the conversation shifted to other topics. Interests. Favorite kinds of music.

Finn was easy to talk with, and the trip to Calgary went quicker than she expected.

Two hours after they left the ranch, they stopped at a tractor dealership on the outskirts of the city. Finn went inside and quickly returned with what he had said he needed. Filters or something? She wasn't sure, but he dropped a box onto the back seat of the truck then got in.

"Now comes the challenge," he said as he pulled out of the dealership, sounding like he was relishing it. "Getting this rig downtown."

"I thought you said you had this under control." She tried not to feel a tiny shiver of guilt.

"Of course I do. I'm a cowboy. We ride anything, anywhere, anytime. Traffic does not faze us."

"Well it fazes me, so I'm glad you're driving."

He chuckled at that, but she said little as he got back onto the freeway leading into the city. What felt like a hundred stop-lights and twenty turns later, he was maneuvering his truck into a tight parking spot by the art store. He blew out a breath when he was done and turned to her, his arm draped over the steering wheel. "See, told you I could park this rig anywhere."

"Duly noted and duly impressed," she said with a grin. "Are you sure you don't mind coming in?" She felt she had to ask. "I'm not sure how long this will take."

"I got time," was all he said. "Don't worry even the smallest moment about it."

With a thankful smile, she stepped out of the truck. As she walked toward the entrance of the store her heart did a little skip of anticipation. And then, when she opened the door, she grinned and pulled in a deep breath, reveling in the smell of oil and the sight of the vast variety of paints and canvases and supplies.

She took a moment to look around, to drink in the sharp aroma of paint blended with a duller scent of paper, canvas, and markers.

Colors everywhere she looked. Paint tubes and pots lined up in rows, channeling the rainbow.

It was a feast for her weary soul.

"Lots of color here," Finn commented, entering the store behind her.

Etta didn't know if he was simply making a remark or if he was giving her a little dig about her color choices. Or lack thereof.

She chose to ignore it, walking slowly down the aisles, resisting the urge to run her hands over the products on the shelves, to touch them and take it all in.

The farther she went into the store, the more her heart filled.

The past couple of months she had forced herself to stay in the house she was renting. To stay focused, pushing through her artistic blocks, trying to stay on task. It had given rise to a sparsity of creative inspiration that she felt now as she walked through the store with its displays, advertising various classes, programs available, showings that were running in various galleries.

Despite the reasons for her being here, she realized that she had needed this.

Badly.

CHAPTER FIVE

S he was smiling. Looking happier than even before the fire. *This place is good for her,* Finn thought as he followed her around the store. She seemed relaxed as she paused by one shelf, then another.

Hard not to keep his eyes off her as her delicate fingers fluttered over the paint tubes, the brushes, the shelves of stuff he couldn't identify.

"Lots of color here," he said.

"Trying to tell me something?"

"No. Not at all. No passive aggression on my part. Merely an observation."

"It's a good observation," she said, her eyes going back to the displays. "Marc Chagall once said, 'All colors are the friends of their neighbors and the lovers of their opposites.' And that's one of the reasons I work in black and white and all the neighbors of them."

"I see that."

"I do incorporate some color in my work," she said, sounding almost a bit defensive. "But I choose one particular color for each piece. To showcase it, so to speak."

He had only seen a few of the paintings she had done and he hadn't noticed any color in them. But he kept his comments to himself.

"Besides, many photographers use black and white. Successful photographers."

Again, that wary and guarded tone.

"I'm sorry, I was just..." He let the sentence trail off as he lifted his hands. "I was just kind of teasing you." He gave her his best apologetic look. The one he saved for Carly when he had overstepped with her.

Thankfully, her expression shifted into a smile. Then she released a chuckle. "I'm sorry. I know how it looks to you, but monochrome has come to be my signature style." She tucked one corner of her lip between her teeth and shrugged. "It's what I'm comfortable doing. And my application for the position is on the strength of that style. It's what I'm best at and, well..." Her words faded off as if she had tried to find one more explanation but lost it.

He held her gaze but at the same time sensed an uncertainty in her tone.

"Can I help you?"

Etta spun around as an older man wearing a loose brown shirt, a layer of wooden beaded necklaces, linen pants, and sandals approached them. He ran his hand through his long graying hair, his wrist holding a plethora of leather bands and more beads.

"Actually, I'm just trying to replenish my art supplies. I lost them all in a fire—" She stopped, and Finn was sure she was thinking about all the paintings she lost. He wanted to move close and give her a hug but sensed it would be improper and probably unwelcome in this public place.

"I'm sorry to hear that," the man said with genuine sympathy in his voice. "My name is Bart, and you are?"

"Etta, and this is Finn."

Bart nodded at Finn, his lips curling just a bit, then he turned back to Etta, dismissing Finn and his cowboy hat and twill shirt. "Which medium do you work in?" he asked her.

"Oil and canvas. Tried and true."

"Any particular brand of paint?"

"I have been using Old Holland Classic, but for now I'm willing to work with Schmincke or Holbein."

"Good choices," he said, approval in his voice. "Thankfully, we got a new shipment of Schmincke in. Lots of vibrant tones and colors. They're over here," he said, lifting a finger to indicate that Etta should follow him. "You say you lost everything, so I imagine you'll need brushes. Do you use a palette knife?"

"Yes. I mostly use brushes for the background and then add layers with a palette knife."

"And which additive do you like to use? Linseed oil or Galkyd medium?"

Finn was lost by now. He followed Etta while they talked about palettes and canvases and birch board, easels, and carryalls and brushes. But he didn't mind. It was fun to see Etta so animated.

Though he had to balk at the prices of some things she picked up. He wondered how the insurance company would work through all of this. While they talked, he pulled out his phone and sent a text to Reuben asking if he'd heard anything from the adjuster yet.

Reuben immediately texted him back. He told Finn the adjuster would give him a rough estimate on the building in the next day or so. The contents would take time because another contractor had to come and evaluate everything. Decide what to clean and what to write off.

They sent a few more texts back and forth and Finn discovered that it could be weeks before Etta would receive any kind of payout on the contents of the house. In the meantime, the pile on the counter kept growing, and the bill grew higher and higher according to Finn's quick calculations. He hoped she could afford it.

He joined Etta and Bart as they discussed the qualities of the various—and expensive—brushes she was buying. More money.

"What do you think, Finn?" Etta asked in a teasing voice, turning to him as he joined them at a long counter. "Any opinions?"

The sparkle in her eye and her taunting tone was a challenge he could not turn down.

"All of this art and inspiration reminds me of an artist joke," he said, trying not to be annoyed at how Bart had been treating him.

"You know an artist joke?" Etta teased.

"Oh, yes. It's about the art thieves who got caught in front of the Louvre." He looked over at Bart. "That's in Paris."

"I know where the Louvre is," Bart said in a tone that sounded like he doubted Finn did.

"Me too. Too many rooms, and Mona Lisa was a major disappointment. Too small and enigmatic. Anyhow…" He dragged the word out, leaning on the counter, borderline flirting with Etta. Make that full-bore flirting with Etta. She was pretty and single, and he was very interested. And he didn't like Bart. "These art thieves were stuck in front of the Louvre with all these paintings when the police caught them. You see, they didn't have the Monet to buy Degas to make the Van Gogh."

Etta sputtered, then laughed out loud.

Then Finn turned to Bart who was chuckling as well, which made him seem less pretentious.

"Actually, I wouldn't mind buying a few things myself," he said to Bart. "I'm a rank beginner. Closest I've come to art was a paint-by-number I did for my mom years ago."

Bart seemed to blanch, but then recovered quickly. "We carry nothing like that."

"But what about if I want to start? What should I get?"

"I can help you with that," Etta put in.

Finn waved her off with a grin. "No. I want color. Lots of colors. I want to paint horses and flowers."

"You better hope the horses stand still long enough for you to do that," Etta said.

"I have very obedient horses. They love to pose," Finn joked.

Etta just shook her head while Bart glanced from Etta to Finn as if not sure how to proceed.

"So what about these?" Finn asked, pointing to a display of tubes of paint across from the cashier's desk.

"Those are good," Bart said. "But might I suggest something a little easier to work with?"

"You might and you should," Finn said, following Bart as he led him to another part of the store.

"Any preferences?" Bart asked.

"No. I'm counting on you to guide me. I don't want to spend a ton of money, but I'd like to have options."

Half an hour and quite a few dollars later, he and Etta were packing large crinkling bags of supplies out of the store and into the back of his truck. It took a few trips, but when he closed the door, he saw Etta looking at the store, as if unsure what to do.

"Forget something?"

"No. It's okay."

"We can go back in. I'm sure Bart is already investing his hard-earned commission or booking a cruise and wouldn't mind if you could give him a chance to upgrade."

Again, her laugh warmed his heart.

"I think I might like to get a few more things," she said.

"Your credit card might not thank you," he joked.

"It won't. I just hope the money comes through quickly from

the insurance."

He just nodded, not wanting to dampen her eagerness.

Bart was surprised to see them again but as willing to help as before. But, to Finn's surprise, Etta walked over to another paint display with her basket and pulled a number of tubes off the shelves.

Blues and reds and greens and yellows and purples and oranges. Colors. A variety of colors.

"Planning to join me in my artistic endeavors?" he joked as she carried the basket to the cashier.

"You will need someone to guide you," she returned.

Bart rang up the next purchase and handed her the bag of paints. "And again, I thank you for your business," he said.

"And we thank you for your patience and help."

"Looking forward to seeing what you end up doing," Bart said to Finn.

"I'll be posting on Instagram." Finn took the bag before Etta could take it and flashed Bart a grin.

The bag joined the others in the back and as they climbed into the truck Etta asked him, "You have an Instagram account?"

"I'm starting one. Hashtag horses and flowers."

"You crack me up."

"Nice to know. And it's nice to see you smiling." He pulled out of the parking space and into city traffic.

"Today is a good day," she returned.

"Today will be a better day for me when we're out of the city."

"I thought you didn't mind driving in the city."

"I don't. Doesn't mean I like it."

She chuckled and looked like she was about to say something more, but her phone dinged and she picked it up. And just like that the smile faded, and it seemed the color drained from her face. She swiped across the screen then dropped her phone back into her purse, her hands shaking.

He waited to see if she would say anything to him, but she turned her head away. The change in her bugged him. She had been happy, lighthearted. Now this.

He knew his brothers would tell him to mind his own business, but he was never very good at either listening to his brothers or minding his own business. More of a full-bore, full-speed-ahead kind of guy. Pick up the pieces later.

"So, everything okay?" he went with, figuring that question was a good balance.

She didn't answer right away which, in effect, answered his question.

"I'll be fine," she said finally.

"Which is in the future." He stopped at a red light and tried not to drum his fingers on the steering wheel, which he often did when stressed. His bluster was coming back to haunt him. Much as he made it sound like it was no big deal to drive an extended cab dually in the city, it was a medium deal at best. The truck was a beast, but the advantage was most of the fancy cars gave him a wide berth when possible.

But she didn't pick up on the small conversational bone he gave her.

So he said nothing, thankful for the chance to concentrate on driving. However, when he pulled onto the freeway leading out of the city, he hoped to pick up where they'd left off. Etta had been twisting and untwisting her purse strap, her fingers worrying at it, her tension like a living thing.

He turned on the cruise control and sat back, feeling much better now.

"So, will you be fine sometime?" he asked, unwilling to let this go.

"I live in hope."

"Did that text have anything to do with the insurance company? I know Reuben gave them your number."

A tight shake of her head was her only reply.

He wanted to find out more, but knew he had to respect her silence. Despite his concern for her, they didn't know each other well enough for him to press the matter further.

But he was sure curious and, if he was honest with himself, concerned.

"Why don't you block her like I told you to?" Annie sounded a little peeved and Etta didn't blame her.

The first time Etta had gotten a phone call from Alistair's wife she didn't recognize the number so she'd answered. When Renate told Etta who she was, Etta cut off the call, unable to talk to the woman whose marriage she had ruined and whose family she had destroyed.

"I should. She hasn't contacted me much lately." Etta put her dirty plate from breakfast in the sink, promising herself she would clean it and the plates from yesterday.

The day before yesterday, on their way back from Calgary, the mechanic had called to tell her that her car was ready. So, Finn dropped her off and now, at least, she had her own transportation.

When she had come back to the ranch, she had set up the easel, put a brand-new canvas on it. While the fabric wasn't the kind she usually used, Bart had assured her she would be just as happy with this brand. If not more. She had laid everything out and turned down yet another offer to join the Sutton family for dinner. Instead she had heated up the leftovers from the meal Adele had brought the day before. It wasn't a whole lot, but enough.

After Renate's attempt to get hold of her, she wasn't that hungry. She'd fallen asleep okay but was wide awake early yesterday morning.

She had some of the yogurt she had bought when she

stopped for groceries. She'd puttered in the cabin, rearranging her supplies and then sketched out her project for the next week. Then she tried to work. But nothing came. She struggled the entire day, sketching, struggling for inspiration.

She hadn't fallen asleep until late. Then, this morning, her sister called to check in.

"When was the last time she tried to call?" Annie asked.

"She sent me a couple of texts after she called and I hung up on her. Then nothing for a while, so I thought I was in the clear. Figured she wasn't interested in contacting me anymore."

"And now she's tried again."

"Yes." Etta pulled her legs up on the couch in the cabin, wrapping one arm around them, resting her elbow on her upraised knees.

"So now it's time to block her."

"I guess." Etta sighed. "It just seems cowardly."

"And hanging up on her and ignoring her texts isn't?"

"I feel like I'm in control if I do that."

"And each time it's generated a huge well of tension."

Etta hugged her knees tighter, acknowledging her sister's comment. When her phone vibrated on the way home from Calgary and she saw Renate's number, it was as if icy fingers trailed down her spine then gripped her stomach. She hadn't been able to stop wondering why Renate wanted to talk to her, imagining an angry wife, a crying wife, an accusing wife. A hurt mother.

Part of Etta wanted to talk to Renate. Wanted to defend herself, but the guilt she felt once she found out Alistair was married was a burden, a struggle she felt she had no right to purge onto Renate.

"You didn't know," Annie reminded her.

Etta sucked in a deep breath, acknowledging that point but still not able to internalize it. To make it her truth.

"Just block her," Annie said. "You've had enough stress in

your life the past while. You need to shed it, to clear your mind and let yourself be absorbed by your work. Find the joy you once had in what you are doing."

"I don't know if it was exactly joy," Etta said, glancing over at the supplies she had laid out on the table in the cabin.

All her brushes stood upright in a jar she had also purchased. Two matching cups for cleaning the brushes stood beside it. She had arranged all the tubes from darkest to lightest, as she usually did. The colored ones she had put to one side, as if afraid they might serve as a tempting distraction.

"Fulfillment then," Annie said. "Joy comes and goes, but feeling like you're expressing yourself and giving other people a conduit for their own emotions is valuable and important. So hang onto that."

"Now the question is, which emotions?"

This netted her a long pause, and she knew Annie was also at a loss.

"Whichever emotions you need to express, I guess. And I'm sorry to cut this short, but I've got a client meeting in twenty minutes I need to get ready for."

"On Saturday?"

"You know me. Eye on the prize. But if it will make you happy, I'm going on a hot date tonight."

"Hot date? Tell me more."

"Not yet. We'll see how things progress. Meantime, keep on keeping on."

"I'll try. Thanks for listening. You're a great big sister." Etta laid her head against the back of the couch and looked up at the ceiling.

"Hmm. Not sure I like how you strung those words, but I'll take the intent of them. And one last comment. Take some advice from that hunky cowboy you've been hanging out with."

"What advice?" Etta ignored the hunky cowboy comment.

Annie had no clue what Finn looked like, but the tag was fitting. Way too fitting, in fact.

"Some more color in your painting and in your life."

"I'm wearing a green and white shirt today," she said.

"Progress," Annie said. "Love you, Sis. Gotta go."

Etta ended the call, wishing she could re-ignite the enthusiasm for painting she'd felt in the store. The excitement she had, at one time, felt at the prospect of starting fresh.

Finn had helped her set everything up. Had kindly assembled her easel and had teased her, yet again, about using all the colors she had bought. How he was getting started soon on his own masterpiece.

He made her laugh and, for a moment, forget the shadow of Renate hanging over her, the thought of the woman and her two children making her stomach clench.

She set her phone aside and picked up her Bible, which had been lying beside her on the couch. She was thankful Carly had found this one for her, and had spent a lot of time reading it, finding solace in the familiar cadence and rhythms of the passages.

She turned again to a passage that had caught her attention this morning from First John, and read it aloud, "'If we claim to be without sin, we deceive ourselves and the truth is not in us. If we confess our sins, he is faithful and just and will forgive us our sins and purify us from all unrighteousness.'"

She knew the passage well. Had read it many times in her life.

But now she read the words over and over, trying to make them a part of her. Trying to find the comfort they offered. She had never claimed to be perfect or without sin and had confessed again and again.

And what about facing Renate?

She faltered as the question seemed to accuse her. She reminded herself that she had to deal with her shortcomings one step at a time, and right now she wasn't in a suitable place to deal with Renate.

"Father, forgive me, I didn't know what I was doing," she whispered, hoping that someday she could say the same to Renate.

But not yet.

She stayed a moment, then pushed herself to her feet and walked over to her canvas. That large, blank, and empty canvas. One of four. She had decided to make her first project with her new supplies, the one still fresh in her mind.

This was always the hardest part. Starting. Before she called Annie, she'd spent some time sketching out concepts of the paintings she'd already done. She'd been working on a series of silhouettes against various skylines. The one she'd been painting before the fire was of an eagle against a sunset, the picture split into four, each one able to stand on its own. Her challenge was to create the sunset in shades of black, gray, and white so that people would be drawn into the wonder of it without the traditional oranges and yellows.

Why do I make this so hard for myself?

The question that had been tormenting her for the past month came again, and once again she fought it back.

You are an artist. This is part of the work you need to do. This is who you are.

And yet…the past few months she'd been struggling to re-create a style that had come so naturally before.

Etta picked up her sketchpad and looked over the pieces she had roughed out, seeing the pictures that had danced through her mind. She had tried to capture them in quick sketches and overall was pleased with what she had done. She knew it wasn't the same as the original work that had been lost in the fire, but maybe it was a bit better.

But trying to transfer it to canvas—that's when she stalled out.

Just start. Do the first thing. Then the next.

She picked up a tube of black paint and squeezed out a curl on the edge of her palette. She reached for the gray, did the same, then white, completing the triangle. She stared at the three blobs circling her palette, picked up her palette brush, scooped some black and smeared it in the middle. Then white, then gray. She swirled the shades around, added some more white.

Then picked up another brush.

She looked at the canvas, trying to imagine the dimensions, the layers she'd need, the proportions. But she couldn't visualize it anymore.

A hard, too-familiar pressure rose in her chest, panic gripping her throat as her hand froze midair.

She wanted to push through, but she didn't dare waste a canvas. She had limited supplies and wasn't sure how much the insurance company would pay for. As it was, she had put an uncomfortably large amount of money on her credit card with no idea when she would get paid out.

She waited, then realized nothing was coming. She meticulously cleaned the paint off her brush, ripped the paper off the palette and threw it away, trying not to think of the waste.

She made herself a cup of tea and sat on the porch swing outside, letting the morning sun wash over her.

She gave the swing a push with her toe, breathing slowly in and out, drawing on the yoga she used to practice to still a heart that beat like a caged bird.

"Hey, soaking up some inspiration?"

Etta jumped, spilling her tea, missing her leg but splashing it all over the porch floor.

"I'm sorry," Finn said, hurrying up the stairs to her cabin. "I didn't mean to scare you. Are you okay? Did you burn yourself?"

"No, I missed." Her already overworked heart wasn't sure which beat to hit.

"Again, so sorry. I thought you saw me. You sure you're okay?" He took the mug from her and looked her over, his concern making her feel better.

"I'm fine. Just need to clean up the tea from the porch floor."

Finn waved her comment off. "It's wood, and it's old, and I'm sure it's had many things spilled on it." He handed back her mug then leaned against the upright of the porch, one hand shoved in the back pocket of his jeans.

"How's it going? Glad to be back at work?"

She felt another flicker of concern at his assumption. "It's not going well, I have to admit."

"I can imagine. You've had a stressful week." He snapped his fingers. "Almost forgot. Reuben got a call from the adjuster. They'll be doing an inventory tomorrow. It'll take them a few days, but they hope to have a figure to you by the end of next week."

Eight days away.

"You look worried," he said. "Do you need money to cover your expenses until the payout comes through?"

"No. I'll be fine." She pulled in another breath, forcing herself to remain calm. She had enough supplies for now and enough money in her savings account to cover her credit card if the payout took longer than expected. Her rent was paid up for the duration of her stay, and she had enough money to cover her student loan payments.

But she needed the artist-in-residence program to come through, and for that, she needed to produce.

The endless cycle.

"I can help you out if you're short," he said.

"I don't need help." The answer came out more harshly than she intended, and she regretted her snappy tone. "I'm sorry. I'm just—"

"Tense. I don't blame you." He shifted, standing straight. "So, are you taking a break from painting?"

"For now."

"Do you want a change of scenery? You've been holed up in that cabin for two days now."

"Technically only one," Etta corrected.

"Still, you probably got enough done that you could use some inspiration for other work."

She didn't bother correcting him. No use bringing up her complete lack of progress. "What kind of inspiration are you talking about?"

"Horses. Flowers. Blue skies and mountain trails."

"You have a one-track mind, don't you?" she teased, chuckling.

"I prefer to think of it as focused. Anyway, I need to check some fences in the upper pastures before we put the cows out. It's an easy ride, and it's a beautiful day. Do you want to come?"

"On a horse?"

"Yep."

"I've never ridden a horse before."

"You'll be in good hands. We've got a few fully bomb-proof horses," he assured her.

"Bombproof. You know this, how? You detonate bombs around your horses regularly?"

He laughed, the full-throated sound reverberating in the quiet and creating a tug of appeal and attraction.

Then their gazes hooked and he grew serious.

Which made the previous feelings settle deeper in her soul.

Part of her mind rang out a warning, but the lonely part of her ignored it.

An appealing, single, and uncomplicated man was inviting her to spend some time with him.

She knew Annie would tell her to say yes.

So she did.

Finn checked the stirrups and snugged up the cinch, making sure everything was secure for Etta. He didn't want to be responsible for anything happening to her on his watch.

She sat on the fence, watching him, her hands resting on the railing on either side of her.

She had pulled her hair back in a loose braid and changed from her paint-smeared pants to some black cotton pants and a white T-shirt. Carrying on the monochrome theme, he'd thought when she showed up at the corrals.

"This horse's name is Prancer, and mine is Dancer."

"As in the reindeer?" Etta asked, a tone of humor in her voice.

"Very observant. But no reflection on their personalities."

"So, no flying?"

He chuckled at that and shook his head. "Their flying days are well behind them. Plodding is their top speed." He checked the headstall and then turned to her. "You'll be fine. I wouldn't put you on an untrustworthy horse."

"Good to know." She jumped down from the fence and rubbed her hands on her thighs. A nervous gesture. He wasn't sure how else to reassure her, but she was game to go riding, so he had to trust that she would be okay.

"I want you to lead Prancer around the corral a few times, just so you two can get acquainted. That way you can feel more comfortable with him."

Etta nodded as Finn handed her the lead rope. "I've looped the reins around the saddle horn, so maybe keep an eye on them to make sure they don't slip off," he told her.

"Will that scare him if it happens?" she asked as she took the rope.

"Nope. He wouldn't even notice, but I don't want him stepping on them if they do slip off. He'll stop, and it'll be almost impossible to move him, he's such a plug."

"That doesn't sound very complimentary," she said, moving away from him, glancing behind her to make sure Prancer was following. The horse was right behind her, head down, looking like he was tolerating this treatment. Finn watched Etta more than the horse, trying to read her body language. She seemed tense the first go-round, but the third time she passed him, he could see she was more relaxed.

"Excellent. You passed the first test. Now I want you to get on him and make a few circles. He's a tall horse, so just lead him to the fence. You can climb on him from there."

Etta frowned, as if wondering how this would go, but she followed his instructions and Prancer came up close to the fence. She was on his back in a few effortless movements. Finn hooked the lead rope around the saddle horn and handed her the reins.

"How do the stirrups feel?"

"Like stirrups?"

"Stand up and let me see how much clearance you have."

She did, and he nodded.

"Looks good. He's neck-reined, so you just need to keep the reins on his neck and put pressure on the opposite side you want him to turn."

Etta caught on quick and soon had Prancer following her commands.

"Quick learner," he said, smiling his encouragement. "You feel comfortable?"

"Yes. I do." She smiled down at him and he felt it again. That little thrill deep in his gut, that hook in his heart that he hadn't felt in years.

"Then let's head out and check some fences."

He checked her saddle once more and the bridle, but all was secure.

A few minutes later they were riding out of the yard and toward the first gate. It swung open with a screech, but neither horse even flicked. His horse pushed it open, and he motioned for Etta to pass them. Dancer knew the drill and turned around so Finn could reach down and latch the gate.

"Neat trick," she said to him when he caught up to her. "That's impressive, opening and closing a gate without having to get off the horse."

"It's mostly being lazy, and it only works with these metal gates. Once we get further up, I'll have to do some actual work and dismount."

She grinned back at him then looked away, her smile changing as she looked at the mountains. "This certainly is God's country," she said, her tone reverential.

"It is. I've been all over the world, but nothing beats the Rocky Mountains."

They rode in silence, the horses' plodding hooves muffled by the grass on the trail.

Etta seemed to grow more comfortable the longer they rode. Prancer was behaving the way he usually did. Plodding along, not shaking his head or overreacting.

Finn relaxed as well, enjoying the sun warming his back, the soft trill of meadowlarks and blackbirds bringing back memories of other rides he'd been on with the family. He felt a tug of melancholy remembering the picnic lunches his mother used to pack for them. How they would get to the upper pastures and stop and spread out the food.

"You okay?" Etta asked. "You look sad."

He shook his head. "No. Just indulging in memories of my mother."

"Where is she?"

"At the risk of sounding corny, probably looking down from heaven at us right now. Telling me I should have brought a better snack for you to eat. She loved packing all kinds of food

69

every time we went on any trip that lasted longer than half an hour."

"I'm sorry to hear that. When did she die?"

"About seventeen, eighteen years ago. I was only ten. Don't have a lot of memories of her, but the ones I do have are pretty clear."

"That must have been hard for your family."

"Hard for my father most of all, having to take care of four kids under the age of thirteen."

"Is he still around?"

"No, he passed away about four years ago." Thoughts of his father launched a surprising twinge of sorrow. "I was gone when it happened. That was hard for the family too."

"It seems every family has their happy and sad stories," Etta said.

"Are your parents still alive?" he asked, glancing over at her.

"My father died when I was little. My mother when I was nineteen."

"Anyone else in your family besides you, Annie and Eli?"

She shot him a curious look, as if surprised he remembered her family, but he didn't sense any discomfort.

"No. That's it."

"And where does Annie live?"

"Vancouver."

"Where you're from."

She nodded, her hair glinting in the sunshine that danced between the leaves of the trees.

"I can't imagine living in the city," he said with a shudder. "Gives me the willies."

"Is that a medical condition?" she asked, teasing him.

"Yes. Non-pathological. Untreatable to date, though some research is being conducted in a lab deep in the deserts of New Mexico. Very hush, hush."

She laughed aloud at that. "You seem to have done your research."

"Google is my friend."

This elicited another chuckle, which softened her features and made it hard to look away. He had always found her pretty but now, with the sun burnishing her hair, her smile natural and relaxed, she was stunning.

And funny. And talented. Different from any of the girls he had dated before. Bimbos, Carly used to call them.

Different from Helen, who Carly also never warmed up to, though she was far from a bimbo.

"How far do we have to ride to get to the fences we need to check?" Etta asked.

"It's just up ahead. We need to get through this copse of trees and then when we bust out into the open. We'll have to go through another gate."

"Will you have to get off your horse this time?"

"Unfortunately, yes."

"How sad for you."

He grinned at that, easing his horse closer to hers. She seemed comfortable enough to take the chance. "Maybe I'll get you to open the gate."

"I wouldn't know how."

"City girl," he taunted.

"Born and raised."

"Have you ever thought about moving away?"

She puckered her lips as if thinking. "I don't know. I'd need a compelling reason."

"So, what do you love about living in Vancouver?" He wasn't sure why he was asking. Feeling her out, he guessed. She was the first girl he'd been interested in, in a long time. He hated to admit that Katrina's unsubtle attempt at matchmaking had the potential to go somewhere.

"That's an interesting question," she said after a lengthy

pause. "I never really thought about it. I've lived in that area my whole life."

"Your whole life in the city?"

"Parts thereof. Mostly in East Van. Annie lives on the North Shore in an apartment. I'll be moving in with her if I get the job I'm working toward."

"Remind me what that is?"

"Artist-in-residence."

"What does that mean?"

"It's a teaching position that gives me an opportunity to work more on my art. And teaching is always an excellent opportunity to understand my process. My...why."

"Why, as in..." he prompted.

"As in motivation for my own work."

He thought of the glimpse he'd gotten of the colorless land-scapes she'd done. "So, what is your why?" He guessed he was probably edging a little too close into personal territory but after spending time together the past few days, he wanted to get to know more about her.

Her silence made him think he might have pushed too hard.

"I'm sorry," he said as they approached the gate. "I didn't mean to pry." He got off his horse, thankful for the chance to give her some space. He dropped Dancer's reins on the ground, cranked open the tightener, and dragged the barbed-wire gate aside. "Just come on through. Dancer will follow, and I'll close it behind you," he said as Etta waited, unsure of what to do.

She nudged her horse, and Prancer heaved out a horsey sigh and plodded through the opening. Just as Finn said, Dancer followed. Finn caught his reins as he passed him and gave a gentle tug to remind him to stop. Then he dragged the gate post over to the latch and closed it off.

He got back on Dancer and joined Etta.

"I've never seen a gate closure like that before," she said as they continued walking.

"Works great. Gives the gate tension but makes it easy to open."

"What is it called?"

Finn frowned, trying to think. "I call it a gate boomer. People at the Farm and Yard seem to know what I need when I say that."

She gave him a quizzical look.

"Small-town store clerks," he said. "They can read minds."

"Remind me to stay away."

"I don't know if they can read city minds. Different language."

Another chuckle. Seriously, hanging around this woman was great for his self-esteem.

"Now I'm in the fence-checking part of this little adventure," Finn said. "That means I have to pay attention."

"What are you looking for?"

"Broken wires. Fence posts down."

She frowned, glancing at his saddle. "But you brought nothing along to fix a fence post."

"That we'll do with the quad and tub trailer to hold all the tools. I brought my fencing pliers and a bunch of staples to nail up any wires that are down." He angled his head back. "In my saddlebags."

"I guess it doesn't take much to keep cows in then," she said.

"Not if the pasture has enough grass. Something else I'm checking with my eagle eyes."

"Multi-tasking. Impressive."

He made a circular motion with the flat of his hand in front of his face. "I'm more than a pretty face, you know."

This time she laughed out loud.

She was even more relaxed now than she was in the paint store.

A few moments later Finn noticed a loose wire. He dismounted, pulled some staples and the hammer out of his saddlebag, and quickly had it tacked up again. The post was still solid. The one just past it was listing, so he grabbed the surveyor's tape he had in the other saddlebag, ripped a piece off, and tied it on the post for future reference.

"That sure stands out, doesn't it?" Etta said.

"Color. It's all about color," he teased as he mounted up again. "Catches attention and brightens up your life."

"Is that an unsubtle dig?"

"Not really, but if you want to take it as such, I can't stop you."

"You don't like my work."

Her comment was straightforward, spoken with no hint of emotion. Just the facts.

"I think you're very talented. I didn't see enough of your work to make a judgment."

"Enough to be ragging on me about using color," she teased.

"Well, okay, there's that."

Another beat of silence that, again, didn't feel the least bit uncomfortable. Finn shot another sideways glance her way, surprised to see her looking at him. Neither looked away as other feelings and reactions showed up. Attraction. Appeal.

And the surprising feeling that this girl was exactly right for him.

The realization was like a jolt of electricity crawling up his spine, sparking his brain. Right now he wanted to close the distance between them. To touch her hand, slip his arm around her shoulder as he had during the fire. But this time with other emotions hovering between them.

He swallowed and then, disappointingly, she turned away.

"I paint in black and white because that's how I was nurtured when I first started painting, like I told you when we were at the art shop. I was told I had a special aptitude for expressing emotions that so many other people suppress. My stark paintings give people an outlet for those emotions."

Finn let her words settle, gave them the space they deserved as he tried to think of what to say back.

"Your own emotions as well?"

Her response was a quick nod.

"I'm going out on a limb here," he continued, "but does your painting style have anything to do with your brother?"

She sucked in a sharp breath. The stark look of pain on her face made him feel terrible.

"I'm sorry," he said, his tone pitched low. "I shouldn't have put that out there."

Etta was looking straight ahead, chin up, as if she was fighting back tears, which made him feel even worse.

"Actually, it does, and you're one of the few people to make that connection," she said, breaking the heavy silence that fell between them. "After he died, I felt like life had no color. Like it had been bleached out of my world. So I started painting in monochrome. Initially, it was therapy. A way of managing my sorrow. But my work caught the eye of my prof in my third year of art school. He was the one who—the one—" She stopped, her hands tight on the reins. Prancer lifted his head, sensing the tension in Etta.

Finn watched, making sure her horse was okay. Prancer wasn't flighty, but horses were sensitive to the moods of their riders. And he wanted nothing to happen on his watch.

"Do you want to walk for a while?" he asked.

He thought she would say no, but to his surprise she nodded, dismounting. She put her hand on her hip, arching her back and groaning.

"Thanks, I'm about ready for a break again," she said. "I'm not used to horseback riding."

"It can be hard on the legs and the behind," Finn said. He wanted to ask her more about this professor. Something about the way she spoke when she brought him up triggered a feeling of unease. Especially when he saw how she tensed up.

"How many years were you in university?" He wanted to keep talking and went with something simple and ordinary.

"It was a four-year program, but then I went for my master's, which extended it another year. I was working on my doctorate when I got offered a chance to apply for an artist-in-residence position."

"Will that make it easier to become a professor?"

"It would help. It would give me great teaching experience."

"Not gonna lie, the thought of all that schooling makes my head ache."

Etta's throaty chuckle created an answering tightening in his chest. Seriously, she was way too appealing.

"What did you want to be when you grew up?" Etta asked.

"At one time I wanted to be a world championship bull rider."

"What happened to that dream?"

"The bulls. They had it in for me, and I sustained one too many injuries. Then, after some major life events, I discovered the traveling bug, which took up a lot of my time."

"Until your near-death experience," Etta said.

"That was just the final nail in the coffin," Finn said. "I'd been feeling restless before that. Kinda lonely, to be honest. Traveling around like that is not conducive to family life."

"And is that what you want now? A family?"

"I think about it. But I have to find the right person." He had to force himself not to glance over at her. Force himself not to consider her as the kind of person he could settle down with. Despite the connection they seemed to share, they were on two different planes. "What about you? Did you ever want a family?"

Things were getting personal, but he didn't mind. It was good to talk about these things with someone besides his brothers.

"At one time I did. But then..." Her voice faded away, and she added a one-shoulder shrug as if dismissing the comment.

"But then?" he prodded, knowing he was walking a fine line.

"But then I knew I didn't deserve that," she said, her voice sounding shaky.

The pain in her voice made him want to find out more, but when she started walking faster, as if outrunning her comment, he knew he had to wait.

"How much further do we need to go?" she asked.

"We can go back if you want. I can finish this another day."

She shook her head. "We're all the way out here, may as well carry on."

He admired her spunk, so he honored her request. "We'll go up this fence line, through another gate, and then work our way back to the ranch. If it's okay with you, I want to stop in about half an hour for a drink and something to eat."

"You packed snacks?" Her teasing tone made him relax. Also made him admire her ability to bounce back from her emotional outburst.

"Mom taught me well," he said, keeping his own voice light-hearted. "It's just water and cookies, but they're from Adele's bakery so they're amazing."

"So Adele runs a bakery and Katrina a greenhouse and your sister is setting up an events center on the ranch. Sounds like your family is an ambitious bunch."

He latched onto her change in topic, and as they walked they chatted about family.

He found out more about her sister and her aunt, who would take care of them from time to time.

He talked about his nieces and nephew, telling her stories about some of the cute things the girls did. He hadn't met Dean until his return from traveling.

It was all very light and easy and relaxed.

But the entire time they walked, her comment about not being deserving stuck like a burr in the back of his mind.

CHAPTER SIX

"What do you think? Feeling inspired?" Finn leaned back against the tree, smiling over at her.

Etta took a sip of her water and shifted to rest against the fallen log she was sitting by.

They sat on a hillside overlooking the river snaking through the valley below. She could hear the burble of the water tumbling over the rocks, the screech of a hawk soaring on an updraft, circling. A light breeze rustled in the trees overhead.

Flowers in shades of yellow, pink, purple, and blue dotted the hillside. All wild, all beautiful.

"It's wonderful," she said, stretching out her sore legs. She was tired and didn't want to admit that she was feeling stiff. Her stomach growled despite the delicious cookies she had just eaten.

"I love coming here," Finn said. "Whenever I got into a fight with my brothers or my dad, I used to saddle up one of the horses and ride to these hills. It always made me feel better."

"Did it make you love your family more?"

He snorted. "I was a teenager. I never admitted to loving my family."

"I used to have the biggest fights with my mother when I was in my teens," Etta said. "She would ask me to do some chore around the house and I would always get angry."

"Did your brother do the same?"

His easy mention of Eli surprised her. Most people, once they found out, pretzeled their conversation to avoid talking about him. Etta knew they meant well, but it still led to an awkwardness and pain she never knew how to bridge.

But Finn didn't seem to be bothered by any of that. It was refreshing and made her appreciate him.

"Eli was a good teen. In fact, I used to get annoyed with him and how he went out of his way to help. I always said he was a suck-up. He said he was just being considerate to make up for my attitude." She laughed at the memory.

"Reuben was like that. I always said he tried too hard. That he wouldn't get a bigger inheritance because of it." He finished the last of his cookie and brushed the crumbs off his pants. "Turned out I was right. He got a quarter share of the ranch, just like I did. Though he did get my dad's roping saddle. Not that I'm bitter." He flashed her a smile to show he was joking.

Once again she was surprised at how casually he spoke about topics most people would consider off limits.

"Is the ranch in all of your names then?" she asked, curious.

"Yep. But Wyatt's been the only one who's been around since Dad died. He and Reuben ranched together for a while. At least until Reuben's wife died. But now Reuben is back and so am I."

"And the ranch generates enough income for all of you?"

"We're making plans to expand. Now that I'm back, Wyatt and Reuben will farm more land and run more cattle. They had rented out some of the pasture the past few years but we'll be using that now. Which means we can run more head. Carly is using her share to build her events center, which will generate income as well."

"Ambitious," she said.

"My dad taught us to work hard and play responsibly. Of course, that lesson never took until now."

Etta had to laugh again. Finn was an interesting man. He seemed to be comfortable with himself. She wondered why no girl had ever snatched him up.

She kept that thought to herself, though. Finn's romantic history was none of her business.

A fly buzzed past her face and she swatted it away then leaned forward, hugging her knees. She pulled in a slow breath, feeling a surprising peace despite her aching legs and tired body. "This is the perfect spot for a sulky teenager to come to decompress."

"How about an uninspired artist?"

"I think it's good for someone like that as well."

"Ready to go back and paint some horses and flowers?"

"You won't let that go, will you," she returned with a chuckle.

"I'm a one-trick pony. But I'm just teasing you."

She looked over the landscape below then pulled out her phone and captured the scene. She took a number of shots, zooming in, then going wide. Then, just for fun, she shifted and caught Finn sitting, relaxed, his cowboy hat pushed back on his head, one leg up, his wrist resting on his knee.

"You should call that one, Cowboy at Rest," he teased.

"Or Contemplative Cowboy."

"Then I should do this." He fisted his one hand, resting it on his forehead, frowning.

"Then I'd have to call it, Cowboy Wondering Where He Left His Horse."

"You should take your show on the road. Guys would be falling all over themselves to date you."

"I've never had a guy fall over himself to date me, can't

imagine why a comedy routine would make that happen." She grinned to show she was teasing, but Finn's expression grew serious.

"I can't believe that."

"That my comedy routine wouldn't have men lining up?"

"That you've never had a guy fall over himself to date you. You're funny and interesting and pretty."

She wanted to make another joke to deflect, but his comment made her mind slither back to Alistair and all the years he had taken up of her life.

"You've had boyfriends?" Finn pressed.

"Pauly Jacobsen kissed me in fifth grade, does that count?"

"I'm sure you've been kissed more than that." He held her gaze, his eyes sparkling, and she felt it again. That tremble of attraction.

He moved a little closer, and she did the same, sensing he was going to kiss her.

And she wanted him to.

An image of Alistair jumped into her mind. And behind that came the crushing guilt.

You're not worthy, and Finn is a complication you can't afford.

"We should get going," she said, jumping up to erase the voice in her head. The accusation that always came with thoughts of what she had done.

"Sure." She couldn't see his face, but she thought she heard disappointment in his voice.

Didn't matter. She had to stay focused. Keep her mind on the goal she'd been working towards since she started her arts program.

Full tenure in the university. And the first step was the artist-in-residence program.

She got on her horse, fumbling with the reins. Finn came to help her, his hand brushing hers, sending unwelcome shivers dancing up and down her spine. Once again, she felt an unreasoning urge to give in to the emotions that supercharged any moment together.

But she couldn't. Shouldn't.

He helped her on the horse and handed her the reins, trying to catch her eye. She kept her focus on the mountains surrounding them, forcing herself to pull in a deep breath.

They rode in quiet for a while and she was thankful for Finn's silence.

"Are you feeling okay?" he finally asked as the trail they were riding on left the trees and she saw the valley the ranch was tucked in below.

"I'm okay," she said, choosing to give him an easy answer.

Which wasn't entirely true. Etta was more tired than she had ever been in her life, but she'd been too proud to say anything the last hour. She knew they were on their way back to the ranch, so it seemed pointless to complain.

Her behind ached and her legs were sore, but she also felt invigorated.

"Then you're tougher than me," he said, shifting in his saddle. "I'm beat."

His admission made her feel much better, though she wondered if he was just trying to make up for that awkward situation awhile back.

"I'm done in," she admitted. "But I'm glad you were the first to say something."

"Ah, competitive too."

"Proud." She returned his grin, thankful for his easy transition to their previous give-and-take.

"One of the seven deadly sins," he said.

"I'm guilty of more than one."

"Can't imagine that," he said.

"You have no idea." She couldn't stop the bitter tone that crept into her voice.

Finn looked like he was about to say something when the sound of an ATV cresting the hill snagged his attention.

Etta could see Carly astride the vehicle, waving at them with one hand.

"Hey, you guys," she called out, stopping the ATV a short distance away and turning it off. The horses didn't seem bothered, but Etta was thankful Carly was being cautious. She was too tired and inexperienced to stop her horse if he spooked.

"What's up?" Finn asked.

"Nothing. I was just out for a ride..." She paused, but Etta could see she was upset.

"Going where?" Finn asked.

"Just around." She sighed, shaking her head. "Need to blow off some steam and I didn't feel like saddling up a horse."

"Probably just as well," Finn said. "You shouldn't be on horseback if you're annoyed. What's up?"

Carly twisted her hands back and forth on the handles of the quad. Finally, she puffed out a heavy sigh. "I just found out my contractor took on another job and is putting me off. Again."

"By how long?"

"He wouldn't say." Carly pressed her lips together then gave Etta an apologetic look. "Sorry. Didn't mean to drag you into my drama. You've had enough of your own lately."

"I'll say," Finn said.

"On that note, I'm glad I caught you," Carly said to Etta, ignoring her brother. "Reuben said he's meeting with the adjuster Monday to hammer out the final details on the claim."

"That's good to know." Etta had checked her bank statement online and tried not to panic. After the huge bill she'd racked up at the art supply store, she knew she wouldn't be able to pay her card down completely. She'd budgeted for eight months of working to get her portfolio together. Not for paying for hundreds of dollars' worth of supplies.

"And Finn, Wyatt said to ask you to come to the shop when

you're back. He needs some help changing the oil on the John Deere tractor."

"Reuben gone?"

"He's helping Katrina at the greenhouse today. She's getting ready for a big sale."

"He's so whipped," Finn said with a shake of his head punctuated with a sigh, but Etta could see he was joking.

"He's a good guy," Carly returned. "Unlike some."

The bitter note in her voice was a surprise, but Etta sensed there was some history behind it.

"Yeah, okay. True enough," Finn said. "Are you going back to the yard?"

"Out for a ride, remember? Trying to work off some frustration, remember?"

"Have a good ride but stay in third, okay?"

Carly waved off his comment but drove slowly away, probably so as not to scare the horses.

"Shall we carry on?" Finn said to Etta. "And don't mind Carly. She's been dealing with a bunch of stuff lately. But then, so have you." He gave her a lopsided smile that she couldn't help but return.

"I'll get through it," she said with more confidence than she felt.

Neither of them spoke on the last leg of the ride. They got to the ranch, and as the horses came to a halt by the hitching post, Etta sat a moment, too tired to even make a move to get out of the saddle. Finn was already off Dancer and had him tied up before she could shift to dismount.

She groaned and then, to her surprise, Finn was beside her, his hands on her waist as he helped her down.

She felt she should protest but, again, didn't have the energy and, if she were honest, no desire. She could be all "I am Woman Hear me Roar," but even a whimper would be too taxing.

And, even more, deep down she liked being helped by a man. Liked feeling taken care of.

And when he set her on the ground, still holding on to her waist, looking down into her eyes, her breath lodged in her chest, her heart pounding. His face was shadowed by the brim of his hat so she couldn't read his expression.

But she didn't have to.

When their lips met it felt natural. Unrushed. Easy.

His mouth slipped over hers and she melted into his embrace, slipping her arms around his neck, her fingers entangling in his hair.

He groaned and pulled her tight against him, his warm body strong and his embrace comforting.

But his kiss, oh his kiss. It ignited emotions she hadn't felt in a long time. Created a yearning to deepen the kiss, to stay here forever. He moved his lips to her cheek, her forehead, then he tucked her head against his neck, his hand holding it in place.

"Oh, girl," he whispered. "You make me crazy."

His words thrilled her, gave her a small feeling of power.

Then his chest lifted in a deep sigh as the sounds of the ranch slowly registered. The birds, the snort of the horses beside them. In the distance, the muffled whine of the ATV as Carly drove away from them.

Etta didn't want to leave his embrace, but as reality entered the moment, she knew she had to pull back.

When she did, he murmured a protest, but she ignored him, her head down, her hands still resting on his shoulders.

"I'm not apologizing for that," he said, his tone matter of fact.

"I don't want you to."

She kept her gaze on the third button of his shirt, focusing on the small grease stain beside it, inhaling the smell of leather and horse underlaid with a piney scent. Finn.

She closed off the chiding voice, the demanding voice, all the voices she knew would tell her this was a mistake and that it was all wrong and that it distracted her from what she needed to do.

Because right now, with this amazing, handsome man, after spending such a wonderful afternoon doing something drastically different from her usual day, she just wanted to let the experience and the attendant emotions settle. She wanted to hold on to them, meld them into her soul. Embed them into her brain.

When the lonely days came back, and they would, she would have at least this to hold on to. A memory to carry her through those empty times.

"I like you." He stroked her cheek with his rough knuckles, his hand coming to rest on her shoulder. "A lot. I haven't felt this way about anyone before."

She wanted to stop him. Didn't want this to be more than it was. A moment with an attractive man. A kiss that she would tuck into a memory box.

But even as he spoke, she caught herself wanting to drift back into his embrace. To kiss him again.

Because whether she wanted to acknowledge it or not, he was seeping into her life.

And she knew she couldn't let that happen. Not again.

"Etta didn't want to come in for dinner?" Carly asked as Finn entered the kitchen.

He hadn't wanted to eat at the ranch house either, but after helping Wyatt with the tractor, they had tackled the haying equipment, replacing teeth on the hay bind and wrestling with a motor that Wyatt wanted to pull out of an old truck and put in another one.

On top of a lengthy horse ride, the physical work had

exhausted him, so when Wyatt invited him to join the family for dinner, he gladly accepted.

Reuben was still in town. Dinner at his own house would have been a sandwich or cold cereal in front of the television. He wasn't ready to be alone with his thoughts.

However, now that he was in the kitchen, facing Carly's questioning look, he wondered if Cheerios might have been a wiser option.

"She wanted to get back to work," he told his sister.

And he sensed she wanted to escape. After the kiss that had truly rocked him off balance, he had hoped to spend some more time with her. Talk. Find out what was going on behind those eyes that could sparkle with laughter and grow dim with sorrow. She intrigued him and he wanted to find out if there could be a next step.

Something he hadn't experienced since Helen. And even then, he knew that he hadn't fallen as hard and fast for Helen the way he had Etta.

He reined in his thoughts as he slid open the door to the family room. Maya and Maria were watching television. The nanny had left half an hour ago and Adele wasn't back from the bakery yet. The television was a convenient stopgap until Wyatt came back into the house.

"Hey, kiddos, what up?"

"Nothing," Maya said, frowning at him. She wore a pink T-shirt with a sequined heart on the front and was running her hands up and down the sequins, which made them change color as she watched. "We just sitting here. Nothing is up."

That he couldn't dispute. Maria lay draped over one end of the couch, and Dean slouched in Wyatt's recliner, his head on his chest, frowning at the iPad in his hand.

"Do any of you want to play a game?" He felt restless, needing to do something. Etta had offered to help him with the horses, but he could tell she had retreated from him. Again. And he didn't want to be that close to her when she was like that.

So he told her he could manage on his own.

She couldn't seem to leave fast enough.

"Nope. I like TV," Maria mumbled. Maya just ignored him, the little stinker. He was tempted to stand in front of them to block their view of the vapid cartoon they were watching, but he knew it would only annoy them.

"What about you, Dean?" Finn turned to his nephew.

Dean didn't answer right away, which gave Finn the answer he needed. He left the kids to their own devices, literally, and went back into the kitchen.

Carly was cooking tonight and from the way the kitchen smelled, pasta, pesto, and spicy sausage was on the menu.

"Need any help?" he asked as Carly chopped up some peppers for the salad she was working on.

"You can set the table."

"For how many?"

"You, me, Adele, Wyatt, and the kids. Reuben and Katrina are eating out tonight."

He pulled the old, worn placemats out of the kitchen drawer. "I remember when Mom made these," he said, setting them on the large, extended table.

"Do you? I can't remember her sewing."

"She made them before she got sick. I was allowed to help her by handing her the colored squares."

"You're a closet tailor then?" Carly teased.

"No. Quilter. Get it right."

Carly's chuckle made Finn think the ride she had taken had done her some good. Lucky her. His outing had only fostered more confusion for him. More tangled emotions he wasn't sure how to sort out.

"So, you and Etta had a good time?" Carly asked, her voice holding a peculiar tone.

Finn glanced over at her but she was cutting up cucumbers now, her expression bland. "Yeah. It was good. I had to staple up a few wires, but the fences are all solid."

"Wyatt and Reuben will be glad to know that," Carly said. "And what about you and Etta? Are the two of you solid?"

Finn yanked open the silverware drawer with a bit more force than necessary. The cutlery rattled and he sucked in a breath to steady himself. "What do you mean?" he countered.

Carly was up to something. Better to return a question with a question in those situations. She'd tricked him too many times into saying too much.

"What do you mean, what do I mean?"

Finn shook his head as he counted out the forks and knives. "Nope. Not doing this."

Carly sighed, "Okay. You can try to be coy, but Dean told me, as soon as I came back from my little ride, that he saw you and Miss Etta kissing in the corrals."

Though Carly was his sister and things like this shouldn't bother him, technically, he still felt a jolt of guilt.

"What are you trying to say?"

"You haven't kissed a girl since Helen."

"And you know this how?" Finn brought the cutlery to the table and set some on each placemat, proud of his control of the conversation.

"You tell me everything. And you never told me about any girl you kissed while you were traveling."

"That's because I didn't."

"To me, that means this Etta is someone special."

Snagged him again. Every time.

"We went riding. You know how romantic that can be." Oh, that was so lame. She would be all over that one. "It was just a kiss."

Carly snorted. The kind of snort a sister can release and say much more than just a simple sound.

"You told me, unequivocally, that after Helen you wouldn't kiss a girl again unless it meant something. So..." Carly turned to face him, holding the knife, angling him a curious look.

He wasn't finishing her sentence. "Do we need spoons?" he asked.

"You're not saying anything, are you?"

"Or should I just leave them in the drawer?"

He didn't look at his sister. He knew she wasn't quitting, but neither was he.

Then, before she could say anything else, the porch door opened and Adele came inside, carrying a few grocery bags and one from the bakery. Goodies for them, no doubt.

"I'll get fat if I eat here too much," Finn joked as she set the bags on the counter.

"Didn't you know? Stuff from my bakery isn't fattening," Adele said as the door of the family room slid open and the kids burst into the room.

"You home," Maria shouted out, running to Adele, her arms wide.

Adele knelt down and scooped the little girl into her arms, giving her a tight hug. Finn grinned at the sight of the kids crowding around her, happy to see her.

The sight gave him a pang. At one time, when he and Helen were engaged, he had imagined a family. A wife and kids living here on the ranch. When he found out she'd been cheating on him, he had initially been devastated. But over time and talking with his family, he realized it was for the best. Last he heard, Helen had been married and divorced already. Though their breakup had started Finn on his traveling, he kept going because he enjoyed it.

Until he didn't.

And now he was ready to settle down. To return to his roots. To make a home.

With Etta?

He shook off that question as he filled the pitcher with ice water. Sure, he was attracted to her. Sure, they had kissed.

But make plans? She was in her cabin now, painting, getting work together for a job that would take her away from here. He had to be realistic.

Then why had she kissed him back?

"Fences all in order?" Wyatt asked as he swung Dean up into his arms.

Finn hadn't noticed his brother coming into the house and startled, almost spilling the water from the pitcher as he turned.

"Jumpy much?" Wyatt joked. He gave Dean a hug, then set him back on the floor.

"He kissed Etta," Carly announced.

Finn shot a glare at his sister, who just shrugged it off.

"I saw him too," Dean said, sounding smug.

"I didn't," Maya announced as if to say, if she hadn't witnessed it, it hadn't happened.

"You were in the barn with the cats," Dean said.

Wyatt frowned at Finn, and he felt like a heel. Wyatt could be such a big brother, which could be annoying. Finn ignored him.

"Can I do anything?" Adele asked Carly, interrupting the conversation.

"Nope. Supper is ready." Carly set a bowl of steaming hot pasta and sausage on the table, followed by a bowl of salad.

A few moments later they all sat down at the table. Wyatt glanced around, just like their dad used to, smiled, and then bowed his head and prayed a blessing on the food, on their work, and on what they were to do that night.

Adele and Carly got the kids' plates ready, and Wyatt cut up the girls' noodles and sausage.

"Smells delicious," Wyatt said, grinning at his sister. "Mom's recipe?"

"Absolutely, but with a twist. I used more pesto than she did."

"And what's for dessert?" Maya asked, looking behind her to the bags Adele had brought in.

"You'll find out when you finish your supper," Adele teased, tapping her on the tip of her nose.

Maya twisted her mouth, not happy with the answer, but she picked up her fork and started eating.

The table talk veered from the ranch to Adele's day at work to the fair Adele was helping with. Carly talked about her struggles with the contractor. The kids talked about the new game the nanny taught them and how excited they were for the fair. Thankfully, no one brought up Finn's now-public kiss.

When supper was over, Adele offered to help with the dishes, but Carly told her and Wyatt to go and sit with the kids in the family room.

Once the door slid shut behind them, Carly turned to Finn as he gathered up the plates. But Finn knew where she was headed and beat her to the draw.

"Tell me about the contractor. What's up with him ducking out on you?"

Carly's eyes narrowed and her lips thinned in anger. Though he felt bad for her, he figured from her response she had been distracted. They wouldn't be talking about Etta.

"He's put me off. Again." She grabbed the pot she had cooked the pasta in and scrubbed the inside before dropping it with a clang into the dishwasher. "I've been getting calls from people wanting to book events for late winter, but that won't happen at the rate this guy is working."

"Can you get another contractor?"

"I doubt it." Carly sighed. "Most of the good contractors are booked out until fall."

"I heard that Crossing Construction lost their contract to build the addition on the school."

"Yeah. I heard that too," Carly said.

"So?"

"That's Derek's brother's company."

"So?"

She glared at him. "Why would I even consider having anything remotely to do with that family?"

Finn understood her anger. Derek, her one-time fiancé, had gone to jail three years ago for possession of cocaine. He had just gotten out a month ago on good behavior, according to the Millars Crossing gossip, or, as Reuben liked to call it, the Millars Crossing Messaging Service. Apparently, he was coming back to town to work with his brother. Derek's youngest brother, Kyle, was dying of lung cancer, and Finn imagined Derek would want to be with him.

"You won't be hiring Derek. Just Kyle," Finn pointed out.

Carly looked down, but despite her anger, Finn caught the glint of tears in her eyes. He wanted to reach out to comfort her but knew Carly wouldn't appreciate it. After Derek went to jail, Carly did the same thing Finn had, the same thing Reuben had after his wife's death, left Millars Crossing. Took some time to adjust her expectations. She refused to talk about Derek, and any time his name came up in conversation, she would either change the subject or become angry.

She had come back a few months ago with a plan to build an events center on the ranch. It had been a lifelong dream of hers and she was determined to see it come to fruition. Except now, things had come to a halt.

"What else are you going to do? You need to get this finished," Finn continued.

"I suppose."

"I remember you poring over websites, gathering pictures from magazines. All for this center."

"Lifelong dream," she said with a light laugh.

"So who cares who makes it come true?" Finn asked as he dropped the last dish into the dishwasher and closed it up.

Carly wrung out the cloth she used to wipe off the counters. "I guess you're right."

"Usually am."

She wiped the counters as Finn turned on the dishwasher. Then she turned to him. "And what about you? What lifelong dream have you had?"

"You're going to ask me about Etta, aren't you?" he said, leaning back, his hands resting on the counter behind him. Figured he may as well get right to the point.

"I was hoping to be a bit more subtle," Carly said, hanging the damp cloth over the kitchen tap.

Finn tapped his fingers against the edge of the counter, not sure what to say. Not sure himself what to think.

"I like her. She's really funny. And she's a thinker."

"And really pretty."

"I hadn't noticed."

"Right."

Finn looked away, his own confusion blending with his changing feelings for Etta. His practical brain told him it wouldn't work.

"And now you've got your thinking face on," Carly said, flicking his arm with her finger. That used to just send him, but right now, it was only a small annoyance.

"I have a functioning brain," he retorted. "It kicks in from time to time."

"I've always known that. And what is that functioning brain thinking?"

"That it's way too soon to be trying to sort everything out."

Carly was quiet, and Finn was about to leave.

"You surprise me," she finally said, holding his gaze. "You usually see something and go for it. Deliberation isn't a word I connect with you."

"I ponder. I debate."

Her disbelieving look gave him pause.

"You often jump in and think later."

"That's how I ended up rock climbing in Thailand and then almost dying."

She was silent, as if remembering that moment for herself. Carly was the first person he'd called from the hospital. She was the one who helped him arrange his flight home.

"It changed things for me. You yelling at me on the phone made me realize that people care." He slanted her a wry smile. "Even if they do use bad language."

"I was scared."

"I know. I got the message, and I listened. But more important, Etta has had some difficult times in her life. And I don't want to treat her as casually as I've treated other women."

"Growth. That's good."

"I can be taught." He scratched his temple with his forefinger, thinking. "Etta is...different. It sounds corny, but I feel a connection with her I never felt with any other girl. There's a depth to her that calls to me. It's just..." He eased out a sigh as the sentence faded away.

"It's just what?" Carly encouraged.

"Her plans don't involve sticking around Millars Crossing. And I can't find my way around that."

Another beat of quiet gave weight to what he had just said.

"Do you think she's attracted to you? That she feels the same?"

"There's a definite connection," he admitted. "I don't think I'm being too conceited to think she's not indifferent to me."

"That's a hard one," Carly admitted. "I wish I could give you some advice on that. Maybe it's best if you back off. Don't get too involved. If it's her career and her dream we're talking about, you don't want to mess that up for her."

"I know." Another sigh. Carly's words were like a wedge in his heart, but he couldn't ignore them. He glanced at the clock and pushed away from the counter. "I better get to bed."

He gave his sister a quick hug. "And you, I hope you get this contractor thing figured out."

"I will. I hope I will."

The note of doubt in her voice made him feel bad for her. He wished he could fix this huge problem, but he knew she would figure it out. Carly was tough.

He gave her a parting smile, then walked out of the house. The sun had set. The windows of Etta's cabin glowed a gentle gold. A shadow paused at the window, as if looking out.

Could she see him?

He stopped, and when she lifted her hand in a wave, he felt an uptick in his heart rate. Silly, he knew, but it was another example of the bond growing between them.

What he would do about it, he wasn't sure.

Etta sat on the church bench, her hands folded over each other. This was the first time she'd come to church since she had moved to Millars Crossing. She'd never felt she had any right to be here. But when Finn asked so casually if she was coming, as if her attending was the most ordinary thing in the world, it triggered something deep in her that yearned to be a part of a church community again. Oh sure, she read her Bible regularly, but the last little while that hadn't been enough to satisfy the deep desire she felt to be closer to God.

"'There is therefore now no condemnation to them which are in Christ Jesus.'"

The pastor paused after reading those words, then looked up at the congregation.

"I read this passage whenever I am struck with guilt over not feeling that I am enough. Over taking on burdens that aren't mine to bear."

His words caught something in Etta. Some deep truth she

hadn't dared acknowledge.

"Yes, we need to know when we've harmed people, but there are times we can get so consumed by guilt that we pull inward. That all we can think about is the things we have done. Guilt can make us turn so inward that instead of turning to Christ, who can help us through our guilt, we punish ourselves and create a cycle of anger and guilt that can drain us. Sometimes we just need to forgive ourselves."

Etta caught what he was saying and struggled to hold on to it. To cling to the promise his words offered.

You have no right to feel happy. You're not innocent.

That snake oil voice slithered into the recesses of her mind.

You didn't know. Her sister's voice rose up as if in opposition.

She closed her eyes as her thoughts engaged in the ongoing battle she'd been fighting in her mind the past half year.

Was it really all that easy? What she had done was huge. She knew what it was like to lose a father. And now she was the one who had caused Alistair's children to lose him in an even harder way...to have Alistair's wife lose her husband...how could she get past that?

Then the pastor announced the final song. Etta shifted her attention to the large screen on one side of the pastor's pulpit where the words of the song were displayed so the congregation could sing along. She didn't sing, but she read the words over and over again.

Lay down your needless burdens,
Christ calls you to him,
Release your pain and sorrow,
Let him heal you again.
Release the guilt you carry,
Release the pain you hold,
Open your heart to Jesus' love,
He seeks to make you whole.

The song was simple, but the repeated use of the word *release* gave her a mental image of unclenching the pain and guilt around her heart.

She was tired of the paralysis all her indecision and guilt was creating. She had prayed for forgiveness endlessly. Maybe the pastor was right. Maybe she was mocking God or not believing Him if she wasn't taking the forgiveness He offered.

She took a deep breath as the song came to a close, and as the final chords of the song echoed in the building, she sent up yet one more prayer. It was unformed and garbled but she knew God would be able to untangle it.

Then as the people exited the church, she followed along. A young woman smiled at her, as if to engage her.

"I don't believe I've seen you here before," the woman said, extending her hand to her, corkscrew curls framing a smiling face. "My name is Alicia Mays."

"I'm Etta Caprice."

"Oh, yes. I've heard about you. You're the artist. That's exciting. How are things going?"

She knew the question was a simple conversational gambit to get things going. But once again it reminded her of how things were *not* going.

"It's been difficult since the fire," Etta admitted.

Alicia placed her hand on her chest, her mouth the perfect O of shock. "That's right. I'd heard about that." She brushed Etta's shoulder lightly, a gesture of sympathy. "Of course you're having difficulty finding inspiration. That's incredibly stressful."

She seemed sincere and truly interested, and Etta felt a moment of connection. "I didn't get hurt," she said. "I wasn't in the house when the fire started."

Alicia shook her head, her curls bouncing. "Well, we can be thankful for that. Where are you staying now?"

"The Suttons have an extra cabin on their ranch that they're willing to put me up in," Etta said.

They moved along, slowly heading out of the church in the wave of humanity.

A voice behind them put in, "Are you the girl that had the fire?" Obviously, she had been listening in.

She glanced back to see a young mother, her baby on the hip. "I heard about that. That must've been scary. I'm glad you're okay. I'm Serena."

Etta didn't know these people at all. She had never met them until today. But their expressions of sympathy created a warmth in her heart.

"I'm okay," she said, repeating her previous assertion.

"But I heard that your paintings were damaged," the woman said.

Etta frowned, surprised she knew.

"Millars Crossing Messaging Service. Stuff moves around quicker than bits and bytes on the phone."

Etta chuckled at that.

They had come to the end of the aisle, and people spread out. A little girl came running up to Alicia waving a piece of paper from her Sunday school class. Someone else caught Serena's attention, and they slowly dispersed with a quick wave and a good-bye. Etta watched them go, feeling a touch of melancholy as Alicia grasped the little girl's hand and Serena handed the baby over to her husband.

Family groups.

At one time she had imagined her and Alistair in the same situation. Married. With children.

She tossed that aside, frustrated that Alistair could still sneak into her thoughts when she had worked so hard at blocking him out.

"Hey, it's good to see you here."

Finn's deep voice behind her gave her heart a quick lift and then an extra beat. She swallowed down the sense of expectancy his presence generated.

His hair was slicked back, its unruly waves tamed, comb marks still evident. He wore a white shirt tucked into black jeans.

"Like my clothes?" he asked, lifting his hand and gesturing from his shoulder down. "I thought you might appreciate the basic black-and-white effect."

"Very elegant," she returned with a grin. "Understated and yet in itself making a statement."

"Very deep. When the reality is it's much easier just to pick a white shirt and black pants. That way I don't get into trouble with my future sisters-in-law."

He came up beside her as they walked through the large open foyer to the doors beyond. He pushed the door open for her gesturing for her to walk through.

"Elegant and helpful," she said.

"Deep down I'm an English gentleman."

"How deep?" Etta teased.

He grinned back at her, and again she was surprised at the ease of their conversation. How she could joke with him? Something she had only ever been able to do with her brother, Eli.

"Now you look sad." Finn drew her aside. "You okay?"

"Lots of people seem to be asking me that lately," Etta said, trying for humor again.

"That's because people care," Finn said. "I guess I care about how your smile turned upside down into a frown so quick?"

She wanted to deflect his simple comment, but suddenly was tired of carrying so many things on her own.

"I was just thinking about my brother, Eli. We used to joke around like this."

She hadn't been looking for sympathy.

But when Finn placed his hand on her shoulder, his thumb making small circles on her neck, her heart went into overdrive.

She swallowed down remnants of what she had felt when they went horseback riding, knowing she was falling for him.

She had to fight the urge to place her hand on his chest, anchoring herself to him.

"I have to say I feel honored that I remind you of your brother," Finn said. "I'm sure, as twins, you two shared a special bond."

Etta nodded, surprised at the sorrow that thickened her throat. His humor, empathy, and understanding brought out the loneliness and sorrow over losing Eli she thought she had dealt with.

"I just want to make sure you know I'm available to talk. Or if you need a shoulder to cry on." Finn tilted his head to one side, as if looking at her from a different angle. "Except not with this shirt. I know you're wearing mascara and I don't want smudges. I have to do my own laundry, you know."

And just like that he managed to pull her from the brink of grief and make her laugh. This guy was almost too good to be true.

Be careful, be cautious. You have your future laid out. Don't get distracted by his appeal.

She wanted to ignore the voice, give in to what was clearly humming between them.

But she had to be realistic. She was about to step away and say good-bye when Katrina joined them.

"Hey, you guys," she said, her voice light and breezy. "Adele told me to find Etta and invite her for Sunday lunch."

Her initial reaction was to say no. Step away from Finn, especially when she caught Katrina's eyes flicker to Finn's hand on her shoulder.

But Finn didn't move. "I think that's a great idea," he said, giving Etta an encouraging smile.

"It won't be peaceful," Katrina warned. "The whole gang'll be there. Adele, Wyatt and the kids, me and Reuben, and of course Finn. He's the rabble-rouser of the family."

"What about Carly?" Finn asked.

Katrina shrugged, raising her hand in a vague gesture. "Reuben said her truck wasn't in the yard when he left for church, so no one's sure where she went." She turned back to Etta. "Please come. The kids want to get to know you better. But if you're not fine with that," she said hurriedly, giving her an out, "then just say no. But I know Adele has been itching to feed you."

"And how could she resist such a gracious invitation?" Finn laughed.

Again Etta had to chuckle. And suddenly the thought of sitting by herself in her cabin held little appeal. "Thank you. That would be nice," she said.

"Excellent," Katrina said. "I'll let Adele know. I know she brought a bunch of stuff from the bakery she'd made for today."

"See, there you go," Finn said to Etta. "Even more incentive to come. Adele makes the best snacks."

"I know," Etta said. "I've bought pastries and bread at her bakery before. Everything was amazing."

"Then we'll see you in a little while," Katrina said before she left.

Throughout their conversation, Finn had left his hand resting on her shoulder. Etta had wanted to pull back, but it would have drawn more attention to it so she had stayed where she was. Now Finn moved in just a little closer, squeezing her shoulder lightly, his eyes delving into hers. "I hope you're okay with this. I know the family can be overwhelming, but overall, we're good people. And to tell you the truth, I wouldn't mind spending a little more time with you."

Etta couldn't keep her eyes off him, couldn't look away. She had to admit she was looking forward to spending more time with him too. "Then I'll see you at the house," was all she could say.

And as she walked to her car, she felt a tickle of expectation that she hadn't experienced in a long time.

CHAPTER SEVEN

"Are you sure you don't need any help?" Finn asked Adele and Katrina as they sliced bread and stirred soup.

Adele waved him off. "Go sit in the family room and make sure Reuben doesn't talk Etta's ear off about the insurance. Not exactly a happy topic on a Sunday."

Finn gladly made his escape. He wasn't handy in the kitchen and had only offered because he felt he should.

Wyatt was out with the kids checking a late cow that was supposed to calve, and Reuben had asked Etta if he could give her an update on the insurance situation. So they had moved to the family room.

"Things are slowly coming together," Reuben was saying as Finn dropped into a chair across from them. "Last I heard, the adjuster has made up her list and will get the final figure to you in a week. Then, hopefully, they can give you some money."

Etta looked tired, and though she was smiling, he also caught the tension on her face as Reuben walked her through the information he had received.

Yesterday, up on the high pastures, she had looked relaxed. Content. Now, not so much. And, like Adele, he wished Reuben didn't think this needed to be discussed right now. Though in fairness to his brother, things were getting busier for him, and he had to take his moments while he could.

"Thanks for all your time," Etta said. "I feel badly that I'm putting you through all this."

"Please don't say that. The fire was in our house, and I want to make sure you're taken care of. I also wanted to let you know that the cleaners are sure they can salvage most of your paintings. It might take a few extra weeks, but they found a company that does art restoration in Calgary. If you don't trust them, we can find another company. Or the insurance company can pay you out."

"How will they value the paintings?" Etta asked.

Reuben blew out his breath and pulled out his phone. "I'll just double-check the e-mail."

Finn watched as she leaned forward, her hands pressed between her knees. She wore light brown flowing pants today with a peach-colored T-shirt and a multi-layered gold necklace. Her hair was pulled back in a clip, tendrils framing her face. Simple yet classy.

And just as appealing as when she wore blue jeans and a paint-spattered T-shirt the day they went riding.

The trip he had hoped would help her, inspire her, but the way she was looking now, he wasn't sure it had. She'd seemed on edge at church, and he wondered if she was thinking about Eli now.

She had a lot going on and he wished he could do more to help her.

"They told me that if you've sold any paintings that would

give them an idea of how to compensate you," Reuben said. "Do you have any idea of what they'd be worth?"

Etta's laugh held a mocking tone. "I've never sold anything, so I'm not sure what value to give them. The paintings were for a job I'm hoping to get. But if they could clean them, that would be best. I'd sooner have the paintings than the money."

"Okay, we'll start with that then." Reuben pulled a card out of his wallet and gave it to her. "This is the company doing the restoration. You can call them to talk about their procedures and ask any questions." He pushed himself off the couch, glancing over at Finn, his lips sliding into a grin. "I should check on Wyatt and the kids. Hope that's okay?"

Finn tried not to react to his brother's blatant attempt to give him and Etta some time alone. Instead he simply nodded.

Etta dragged her hands over her face as she leaned back in her chair. Then her gaze slid over to his and once again, that spark of awareness flickered between them. For a moment he felt as confused as she looked.

He knew he should look away, but he couldn't.

"That would be good if they can restore the paintings, right?" he asked.

"That would be ideal. I can't think of doing them all over again. They just wouldn't be the same."

He didn't think that would be a bad thing, but he kept his comment to himself. It still surprised him that someone with Etta's sense of humor had such a dark outlook on life.

"I noticed you were burning the midnight oil last night," he commented. "Did you get any work done?"

Etta wrinkled her nose and shook her head. "Mostly I just stood and stared at the canvas trying not to think how sore I was from riding."

"That's too bad. I was hoping our trip up into the hills would inspire you."

"It was beautiful, and I enjoyed it," she said, sending a faint smile his way. And again, their eyes locked and again he felt that surge of connection.

He got up and sat down beside her, covering her hands with his. "I'm glad you did. We can do it again any time."

"Don't you have to do ranch stuff?"

"Yeah, but I'm the irresponsible third child who marches to his own drumbeat. It's expected of me to flake out from time to time."

Her chuckle made him grin.

"I don't want to cause any conflict between you and your brothers."

"That conflict was established years ago," he said, lifting her hand and twining his fingers through hers. A casual connection that felt anything but.

She returned his pressure, looking down at their hands. "You're lucky to have your family all around," she said.

"I am. One reason I moved back here." He thought of the job she was headed to back in Vancouver. "And I'm glad to be back with my family. You must miss your sister from time to time."

"I do. I wish we were closer."

"And you will be when you move to Vancouver." He tried to throw the words out casually, wishing they didn't matter so much. Even the simple act of holding her hand, feeling close to her right now, was a reminder of what he stood to lose when that happened.

You need to pull back. You need to pull away. This is happening too fast.

"If I get accepted," she said. Then gave him what looked, to him, like an apologetic smile. "And that's not a for certain."

"And if you don't?"

She held his gaze a beat longer, as if seeking something from him, but then she blinked, and it was gone.

"I guess I'll deal with that when the time comes," she said, looking away and withdrawing her hand from his.

Her withdrawal was gentle, but it was a strong reminder to him of the tenuous reality of their situation.

Her end goal was leaving. His was staying.

⟨❦⟩

"That was delicious," Etta said as she wiped her mouth, hoping she caught the remnants of the creamy cheesecake she'd just finished. "I haven't had cheesecake this good since...well...I can't remember when I've had cheesecake this good."

She realized how silly she sounded and blamed it on a pair of brown eyes that had latched onto her ever since she sat down. She'd tried to avoid his steady gaze, but there was an undeniable magnetism she couldn't resist.

"I'll take that as a compliment." Adele's warm smile made Etta feel marginally less dumb.

"Adele's cheesecake has a tendency to leave people speechless," Reuben added, scraping the last bits off his own plate.

"Well, thank you, Reuben," Adele said.

"I'll third that," Finn put in. He leaned back in his chair, patting his stomach in a gesture of satisfaction. "The whole lunch was great."

"A group effort," Adele said, slanting a smile toward Katrina. "The soup was also delicious."

"Thanks," Katrina said. Then she frowned as a phone sent out a text tone. "Oh brother, I wonder what's going wrong at the greenhouse now," she grumbled. She pushed her chair back and walked over to the deacon's bench just inside the kitchen. She rummaged through her purse and pulled her phone out, then frowned.

"Trouble?" Reuben asked.

"Yes. Francine said she stopped by the greenhouse after work and that water hose we thought was fixed is leaking all over the floor." This was followed by a heavy sigh and an apolo-

107

getic look to Adele. "Sorry, Adele. I have to sort this out. I'll be heading back to my apartment afterward, so I'll say good-bye now." She gave Adele a quick hug.

"I'll come with you," Reuben said, getting up and following her out the door.

Wyatt got up to clear the table, motioning for Adele to sit down again. "Finn can help me," he said, resting his hand on her shoulder. His understated expression of affection made Etta smile.

"I should go home as well," Adele said with obvious reluctance. "I have a bunch of stuff to work on for the fair. I've had to shuffle a few things around. Again."

"I told you not to get suckered into that," Wyatt said with a shake of his head as he gathered up the plates.

Etta made a move to get up, but Wyatt waved her away. "Just stay put," he told her. "You're more helpful than Finn, but we're still hoping to domesticate him."

"You make me sound like a dog," Finn grumbled, but Etta could tell he was joking.

"Just a big puppy," Adele put in, sharing a smile with Wyatt as he leaned past her to pick up some more plates.

Though Adele and Wyatt weren't married or living in the same house yet, there was an ease with how they interacted with each other.

The way a relationship should be.

Her thoughts, unwilling, shifted to her and Alistair. How hush-hush it was. How she could never hold his hand in public or act like any other couple. She knew the real reason now, but seeing Adele and Wyatt, as well as Reuben and Katrina, interact, she knew this was what she wanted. An easy camaraderie. A comfort.

Her gaze shifted to Finn who was now rinsing off the dishes, a dish towel hanging over his shoulder. It was a good look on him.

Then, as if he sensed her gaze, he looked back over his shoulder, again snagging her gaze.

"My dad said you're an artist."

Dean's voice broke into the moment and she dragged her attention to the little boy who stood in front of her, his arms wrapped around a sketchbook, head tilted shyly to one side.

"I guess I am," she said. Even after all these years, every time, she still struggled with a feeling of being an imposter. As if she couldn't claim that title.

"There's no guessing," Finn put in. "She's the real deal."

His affirmation made her cheeks flush.

"Can you teach me how to draw?"

"Me too," Maria put in handing her a pencil. "My daddy sharpened this for me."

"I sharpened it for you to draw with it in your own sketchbook by yourself, not for Miss Etta to do it for you," Wyatt said as he finished putting dishes in the dishwasher. "Just leave her alone. It's Sunday."

"But drawing isn't hard work," Maya put in, also holding a sketchbook.

Etta was tired. She hadn't slept well last night. The sermon had been emotionally draining. But she found she didn't want to leave. It was fun to be part of an easy family interaction. Conversation that shifted and doubled back, interruptions from kids, and non-sequiturs.

"I don't mind," Etta said. Besides, she could hardly turn down those adorable faces. She took Dean's proffered sketchbook.

"I don't know if it's the kind you use," he said. "But my daddy bought it for me at a craft store."

Etta recognized the brand of sketchpad as the same kind she had started on. She ran her hands over the moment, drawing out memories of herself as a child sitting cross-legged on her bed, endlessly sketching and copying from magazines and pictures on the Internet.

"It's perfect," she said to Dean, giving him a smile.

Maya handed her the pencil. "Is this perfect too?"

It was a classic 2H pencil. "It's what I always use," Etta said.

Maria, not to be undone, handed her a blocky eraser, half black, half gray.

"Do you use this one too?"

"Always. It's a great eraser."

Etta glanced up to see Adele smiling at the four of them, and then, again, her gaze crept to Finn's and locked.

The connection was the span of a breath, but the moment drew a sense of unexpected longing. Seeing him with his family showed him as more than a freewheeling joker. He truly loved his family, and they truly loved him. It created another unwelcome ache of longing. A desire to be a part of a family again.

And a desire to be with a good man.

Maya put her hand on Etta's, catching her attention. "Where do you want us to sit so you can show us?"

"I only have one pencil, so why don't you all gather around and I can show you a few things first," Etta said.

"I can get more pencils," Maria offered, then ran off to do just that. Etta opened the sketchpad as Dean and Maya plopped on chairs on either side of her.

As she flipped the cardboard cover, she felt that tiny rush she always did when confronted with an empty page and the possibilities it represented. Somehow this was far less threatening than the blank canvas standing on the easel in the cabin.

When Maria came back, she was frowning at them. "Where do I sit?"

"Why don't you sit beside Maya," Adele said, coming to join them. "And then you can switch places."

"What about Finn and Daddy? Where will they sit?"

"I can sit here," Finn said, pulling out a chair and sitting down beside Dean. "When you and Maria switch, then Dean and I will."

Though she felt his eyes on her, this time Etta didn't look his way. She sensed what he was doing. And the reality was, his subtle flirting made her feel better than she ought. She should shut it down, but with Adele and Wyatt watching, saying anything would draw too much attention.

"Now, I need something to draw, to get you started," Etta said.

"Do a picture of Daddy," Maria called out.

"Nope. I'm fine," Wyatt protested.

"I think it's a great idea," Adele put in. We can see the true you. Or at least the you that Etta sees."

"You can see that without me posing for an art class," he grumbled, but Etta sensed he was just joking.

"Daddy, sit down." Maria jumped up and caught Wyatt by the arm, dragging him over to the table.

He chuckled, ruffled her hair, then did exactly that.

"Trust me, I'll be kind," Etta said.

Wyatt shrugged, then with a screech of the chair getting pulled back, sat down, crossing his arms over his chest.

"The first thing I need to do is start with a basic shape. I'll start with a circle, actually more of an oval. That will be your daddy's face. Then I need to make sure I put all the parts of his face in the right place. So I draw a line up and down and then across the middle of the circle."

"You said it's an oval," Maya corrected.

"Of course," Etta said, grinning at her little art critic. She made a couple of quick lines with the pencil.

"That doesn't look like our daddy," Maya complained.

"I'm just getting started. I'm trying to teach you."

"Just draw him," Maya put in.

"I thought you wanted to learn how to do this," Etta said.

"We have learned over time that it is best to follow Maya's

edicts," Finn said quietly, resting his arm across the back of Dean's chair. His fingers brushed her arm, and she wondered if it was intentional.

She dragged her attention back to Wyatt, her eyes flitting from him to the sketchpad. She looked at him, objectively. Catching the lines of his face, how the light fell on it. The shadows.

Then she began sketching, the pencil's scratch over the paper creating that wonderful sense of freedom. Sketching out her studies for her artwork had always been her favorite part. She felt free. Unfettered. Low commitment and high satisfaction.

A few moments later, she held it up to show the kids.

"That's exactly my daddy," Dean said, clapping his hands. "But you made him look a little funny."

"Great, I've opened myself up to ridicule," Wyatt said with a frown.

Adele got up and stood behind Etta.

"Oh my goodness," she said, her voice full of admiration. "You got him exactly."

Her admiration warmed Etta's insecure artistic soul.

But when Finn leaned over to have a better look, his hands now definitely resting on her shoulder, her soul warmed with something much more than thankfulness. She swallowed, half wishing he would stop, yet surprised at how right it felt.

"That is truly amazing," he said.

Somehow his praise made her feel even better than Adele's did.

"I didn't think you could make that ugly mug look so...interesting," he added.

At that, Wyatt pushed his chair back with a screech and strode over. "Let me see this."

He stood beside Adele, but Etta couldn't look up at him to catch his reaction. She had done many such character sketches in her classes, and often the recipient didn't appreciate the end result.

"Do I really scowl like that?" Wyatt asked. But his voice held more curiosity than condemnation.

"Only when someone is trying to sketch you," Adele joked.

"Do me, do me." Maria scooted over to the chair Wyatt had been sitting in. She dropped into it, grinning at Etta, her hands braced on either side of the chair as if preparing herself for an adventure.

"Don't you want to draw?"

"Just draw me," Maria said.

Etta flipped the sketchpad to a fresh page and studied Maria, figuring out her defining features, then quickly sketched her as well.

"That is truly incredible," Adele said, her voice filled with admiration as Etta worked. "I can't believe how you've captured her so perfectly."

"Like I told you, she's an artist," Finn said. His finger idly stroked her skin just above her T-shirt collar.

Etta knew she should shrug him off, stop this. But the self-discipline she had been exerting the past year was exhausting. What did it matter if she gave in to the gentle flirtation Finn was offering her? She was leaving, and it would give her something to feed her lonely soul when she was back in Vancouver.

She stayed where she was, but she did not look over at him.

Maya insisted on having her turn as well, and then Dean. The whole time she worked, Finn stayed where he was, his fingers on her neck with Adele and Wyatt looking on.

Surprisingly, she wasn't uncomfortable with their scrutiny. She was just fooling around, having fun.

She had to smile at that. It had been a long time since her art had been fun.

After she was done drawing Dean, she handed each of the children their sketches.

"Those should be framed," Wyatt said when the kids showed him their portraits. "I've never seen such a great rendering of the kids."

"They're just a quick study," Etta said, surprised again at the admiration in his voice. "I generally make my sketches more in-depth."

"Yes, we should frame them," Adele agreed, standing beside him. She took Maria's portrait from her. "I'm amazed. Stunned, actually. And how quickly you did it."

Adele pressed her lips together then sat down beside Etta, her elbow on the table.

"Uh oh," Finn said, a warning tone in his voice. "Adele has her 'I have an idea' look on her face."

"I know you're busy with your artwork…" Adele seemed to hesitate, biting her lip.

"Giving you advance warning," Finn said to Etta, his hand now resting on her shoulder. "You're allowed to say no to whatever question I can guess is forming in Adele's mind."

"Of course she is, but let me give her something to say no to," Adele said, frowning at her future brother-in-law.

"Just laying out her options," Finn said. "I know that look in your eyes. It usually means work or a favor."

"Ignore him." Adele flapped her hand at him, but Etta heard a note of laughter in her voice. "I'm on the board for the fair," she continued, turning her attention back to Etta. "Which, I found out, often happens to the new people in town. Anyhow, I'm enjoying it, but I was thinking, as I was watching you work and how fast you work, how cool it would be to have a booth where you could do sketches of people for a few dollars. Obviously, we would supply everything you need unless you have specialty supplies, but do you think you'd be willing to spend half a day doing that? We would gladly pay you."

"And let me emphasize, you are allowed to say no," Finn said, his finger once again stroking her neck, still sending those fun little shivers dancing into her brain.

"When is the fair?" Etta asked.

Adele gave her a sheepish look. "This Friday? I know it's last minute, but what you do won't require a lot of setting up."

"You sound like you're not sure about that," Finn teased.

"Can you just let Adele deal with this," Wyatt said. He sounded very much the older brother, and again Etta grinned at the family interaction.

"I'm trying not to be aggressive and needy," Adele returned, a note of reprimand in her voice. "Just let me... Let me try to find a polite way to do this," she said.

"Sorry, Adele," Finn said. "I'll leave you to do your begging in peace."

"I'm not exactly begging," Adele corrected, turning back to Etta. "And I know, like I said, that you're busy. Of course you can say no. But it might be an opportunity for you as well. Inspiration and all that? Finn said you're struggling with your painting."

"Oversharing," Finn said.

"Duly noted," Adele said.

Etta felt like she should be concerned Finn's family talked about her behind her back. However, even spending the little time she had with them, she knew they were a loving and caring family. And another small part of her soul felt good that they cared enough about her to talk about her.

"I don't know if what I'm doing is what you'd want," Etta said, looking down at the sketches. "They're pretty basic."

"They're perfect."

"Trouble is you'd have to charge at least a thousand a pop," Finn put in. "After all, she's a famous artist."

Etta chuckled at Finn's defense of her. "Thanks for the over-inflated affirmation of the value of my work," she said, finally daring to glance over at Finn, who was looking directly at her.

"You need to value yourself," Finn put in.

"These will take minutes. And I think it would be fun." And the challenge would be good for her. She remembered art sprints she and her classmates participated in. They would challenge themselves to do a determined number of pieces in an hour. Despite the occasional frustration and pressure, she had always been surprised at what had come out of those sprints. Fresh and unique pieces that slipped past her critical self and onto the paper or canvas. "I'll do it. Gladly. And we need to make it affordable so I'll only charge ten dollars per sitting. That should be more than enough to cover the supplies."

Adele clasped her hands over her heart, grinning. "That's amazing. That would be awesome. But I'll talk to the fair organizers about the price. I think it should be higher."

"How do you want this to work?" Etta asked.

"I have to talk to the rest of the people on the board. But I was thinking if you could show up at noon on Friday that would be perfect."

Etta thought a moment then nodded. That was the end of the week. Easier to make a commitment to something that far away. "I can manage that."

"I don't want you to feel like we have to take up your whole day. I know I'm asking a lot, but I can't tell you how much I appreciate this. It would be such a fun thing for the kids."

"And the adults," Wyatt added, still holding the sketch of himself. "I think a lot of people would want a sketch of themselves. Or maybe family portraits."

"Whoa, don't make this bigger than my vision," Adele teased.

"You always say to dream big," Wyatt teased back.

"That's why I'm marrying you," she returned.

Etta listened to their give-and-take, again fighting down a beat of envy. What they had was what she had always yearned for. Especially after losing Eli, the only person who fully understood her humor.

And even as that thought formulated, she had to resist looking over at Finn.

Someone she clicked with in ways she had never with Alistair or any other man she had ever dated.

"I'll let you know when I find out more," Adele said. "Finn said he went with you to an art supply store. Give me the name, and if you give me a list of what you'll need I can pick that up."

Her first instinct was to protest, but she knew she didn't have enough sketchpads. Besides, if they were charging money, she would need to go with a higher quality paper.

"Okay. I'll get that together. I guess a lot depends on how many sketches you'll think I'll be doing."

"I'm thinking you'll be working steady," Finn said.

Again, his support surrounded her, creating a sense of well-being she hadn't experienced in a long time.

And behind that, a warning not to let herself get pulled into his charm and wooed by his affirmations.

"I should go," she said suddenly, setting the sketchpad down and giving Adele an apologetic look. "Thanks again for lunch. It was wonderful." She looked over at the kids. "We can do some more art lessons another time, okay?"

"Of course," Adele said, resting her hands on Dean's shoulder, as he looked like he was about to protest. "Miss Etta has done enough and probably has her own work to do."

"I'll walk you back to your cabin," Finn said, getting up.

"I'm fine. It's only a few hundred feet." Etta avoided his gaze as she stood, pushing her chair under the table.

"A lot can happen in a short time," he teased.

Which was exactly what she was afraid of.

"No. I'm good." And before he could say anything more, she said a quick good-bye and left, her thoughts a battle of what she yearned for and what she needed to do.

CHAPTER EIGHT

"Is everything okay with Etta?" Wyatt asked as he tightened the bolt on the hay bind.

"I hope so." Finn took the wrench from Wyatt and set it back in the toolbox. The past few days they were getting the tractor and haying equipment ready. They wouldn't have to cut for at least a week but they still had some pasture fences to repair after his and Etta's trip up into the mountains.

That seemed like a lifetime ago instead of only three days.

"I haven't seen her for a while, so I'm not sure."

Sunday, he thought they were moving closer to each other. But Monday and Tuesday she had holed up in her cabin. Probably working. He knew he couldn't just barge inside and demand to know what was going on.

Carly had asked Etta to join them for dinner Monday night, but she had declined. He had thought, initially, it was because Adele and Katrina were staying in town. But last night, when

Adele came for dinner, Carly had invited her again and Etta had turned them down again.

She hadn't even been sitting on her deck like she had when he had invited her to go horseback riding. Maybe she was afraid he would do it again.

"You think maybe you should check in on her?" Wyatt asked.

"Carly's been chatting with her," Finn said, bending over to fit a screw in the hay bind's cover.

"I know. But I thought you and her were kind of, you know, getting close?"

Finn wanted to shut the conversation down, but he was also struggling with how things had progressed, or rather digressed with him and Etta.

"I thought so too," he said, tightening the screw with a few quick twists. "But she seems to have retreated. I think she's giving me a message to back off."

"Since when has that stopped you before? You used to see that as a challenge."

"I didn't see Helen as a challenge when she cheated on me," Finn returned, tightening the next screw with a harsh twist.

"That was a clear message I'd say, and hardly the same thing."

Finn didn't bother to reply and checked the next few screws.

"But I see how you and Etta get along," Wyatt continued. "I feel like there's something between you I've never seen with other women you dated. Not even Helen."

"You never liked Helen." Finn walked over to the toolbox to drop the screwdriver in. He grabbed a can of oil and brought it back just as Wyatt pulled himself out from under the hay bind. He stood, brushing the hay dust off his pants, and took the oil from Finn.

"It was mutual, and for good reason. Helen wasn't wife material, and I think you always knew that. But I like Etta. She seems sweet and fun, and I think she gets your weird sense of humor."

Wyatt's comment surprised him.

"I like her too," he admitted as Wyatt sprayed the oil on the exposed gears.

"What's holding you back?" Wyatt set the can down and leaned back against the piece of machinery and folded his arms over his chest, looking like he was settling in for a chat. "Like I said, you never balked from going after what you wanted before."

"Well, it's simple, actually. Right now she's painting up a storm, at least I think she is. Getting stuff ready for this job she's hoping to get. In Vancouver."

"I didn't know it was in Vancouver."

"Yup. And she's got her heart set on it. At least that's the impression I got when we talked."

"That complicates things."

"It does."

"But you like her."

"A lot," he admitted.

"So, would you move to Vancouver?"

"I don't think things have progressed that far," Finn said.

"Maybe not, but at this stage of your life I don't think you're into casual connections anymore."

"I'm not."

"What do you want?"

Finn held that question, letting it settle in the silence. Outside a robin tweeted. A spring breeze rustled through the trees. The sun slanted into the shop through the large open door and the green pastures undulated toward the hazy, still-snow-capped mountains beyond.

"This. I want this," Finn said, turning from the view back to his brother. "I want what you have with Adele. A partnership that allows you to be here and her to follow her dreams. Like what Reuben and Katrina have. I don't want to move again. I've had enough running around to satisfy me for a lifetime. I want to settle here, at the ranch. Make a home here."

"And that won't work with Etta."

"She's an artist. This job is something she's been working toward. A dream come true, she told me. Which means our dreams don't mesh."

"And you wouldn't move to Vancouver?"

"Not sure I'd consider that," Finn admitted, though even as he spoke he felt a pang of regret. "I've only just met her. I mean, how long before you knew Adele was the one you wanted to be with?"

"We were forced together when she brought Dean here," Wyatt said. "But I knew pretty quick. We had our struggles. She wasn't supposed to be sticking around either. But her plans changed."

"I can't see Etta doing what she wants to do here in Millars Crossing," Finn said.

"You never know how things work out," Wyatt said with a shrug.

"Maybe not. But I know I can't risk getting involved with someone who's not sticking around." He turned back to the tool cabinet. "So, what are we doing next?"

Wyatt was silent a moment, then he sighed and straightened. "We can move this out. We're done with it. I want to check over the baler next."

Finn nodded and closed the drawer of the tool chest. He strode over to the tractor, but before he climbed in, his eyes slid over to Etta's cabin.

To his surprise, she sat on the porch swing, her sketchpad on her lap, looking out over the ranch.

He wanted to wave to her. Acknowledge her presence. But his conversation with Wyatt was a stark reminder of the dangers of letting himself get too comfortable with her.

Too close.

He climbed into the tractor, started it, and backed it up to the hay bind. Better focus on the work he had to do.

Etta thought sitting out on the deck previously would inspire her now.

Though, if she were honest with herself, she had done so as much to catch a glimpse of Finn.

She knew he was busy working on equipment. At least that's what Carly told her when she invited Etta for dinner.

It had been difficult to turn her down.

Sunday had been far too enjoyable. Spending time with Finn and his family had given her a glimpse of his life, and part of her yearned for that herself.

And part of her genuinely enjoyed being around him.

But that was a dangerous game. So she had retreated. Played it cool. Kept to herself.

However, two days of staring at a blank canvas, trying to fight her growing feelings for Finn, had been draining.

She'd gone to town one day. Gone for a walk. Messaged Annie. Complained via Facebook to a couple of fellow alumni about how hard it was to get inspired.

None of it helped.

She had finally forced herself to do the work. To acknowledge the resistance for what it was.

Fear.

Now she had come inside and here she was, still staring at the blankest of canvases, her paintbrush loaded with gray paint, waiting for inspiration. She knew what she wanted to do, but unexpected and unwelcome second thoughts stifled her. Normally she would just start painting and let the work speak to her and guide her. Whenever she tried to explain her process to someone else, she often got confused looks.

Which only fueled her indecision. She was applying for a position where she was supposed to be the one guiding and explaining. Helping students express themselves. If she couldn't explain her own process, how was she supposed to teach?

She shook off the doubts and closed her eyes, imagining the picture she wanted to paint.

Mistake.

In her mind's eye she saw Finn astride a horse, pointing out how the hills, with their fresh green, rolled towards the mountains. How the river below them glinted in the sun. He showed her a spot where a horse bucked him off, forcing him to walk back to the ranch. He laughed when he told the story, but at the time he had only been twelve years old.

She saw him climbing into the tractor, pulling himself up, his T-shirt stained with grease, his hair unruly.

And mouthwateringly attractive.

She gripped her paintbrush, took in a breath.

Concentrate. Close your eyes and imagine what you'll paint. Think of the sketches.

But even as the image returned, she didn't see it in the shades of gray, black, and white. The picture revealed itself to her full of color and light.

And flowers.

Sighing, she opened her eyes again. That wasn't working either.

Just start. Put something on that expensive canvas you bought.

With Finn.

Sucking in a deep breath, pushing Finn's presence to the back of her mind, she swirled the paint onto the white canvas, her hand twisting and sculpting the paint. No more blank canvas. Next step. Black. She shaded the swirl she had just made, trying to let it speak to her. Guide her next move.

Keeping her eye on what she had just done, she grabbed

another tube of paint. She squeezed it onto her palette then realized, with a start, she had chosen blue.

She was about to put it back then figured, why not? Maybe if she tried something different, inspiration would follow. She could always paint over it.

The blue blob on her palette made her smile. She picked a red tube and squeezed it on as well, moving decisively as if blocking herself from changing her mind. She grabbed a new brush and blended the colors together and followed the same curve she had just put on the canvas. She frowned at the muddy mess. More red. Possibly a hint of yellow. She plucked another brush out of her container and let the colors decide where they were going. She had painted in color before. This was nothing new. Just unfamiliar after so many years of following Alistair's guidance. Following her own emotions.

Maybe she just needed to get this out of her system.

Maybe she needed to paint mountains, horses, and flowers.

She smiled as Finn's comment slipped into her mind.

Maybe she needed some music.

She turned her phone on and connected it to the small Bluetooth speaker she had bought. But the somber tones of Agnus Dei singing Barber, though hauntingly beautiful, seemed off and didn't fit the setting or her current mood. She scrolled through her songs and then on impulse pressed Play on the playlist that Annie had, for a joke, loaded onto her phone before she came out here.

"You're going to cowboy country, that means you need to listen to cowboy songs," she had said.

It was a joke, something they had both laughed at. But now?

She thought of the songs that Finn played when they drove to Calgary. The catchy beat and harmony and plays on words had made her smile.

She tapped her toe in time to the beat of the first song coming out of the speaker. She was just going to have fun with this. A creative outlet. That was all this would be. Let go and see what happens.

Two hours later, she stepped back from the canvas and smiled. The vague outlines of a horse superimposed against the craggy granite of the mountain peak topped with white shaded in gray. She had put a rider on the horse, barely discernible, a ghost rider. But he had broad shoulders and long hair sticking out of the back of his cowboy hat.

Finn.

Anyone looking at the painting would see a vague silhouette of a cowboy against the mountains. The oils she used gave it a heavier look than she would've liked.

Maybe she should try watercolor? It would create a softer look. More elusive. It wasn't bright and cheerful, but the piece had more color than her previous ones.

She added a few more touches to the canvas and set it aside. She cleaned her brushes, washing them and laying them out to dry. It felt good, and to her surprise, she was happy with what she had created. Not something she would submit for the artist-in-residence, but it brought out another side of her artistic nature that generated a shiver of anticipation she hadn't felt in a long time.

She placed another blank canvas on the easel and on a whim took out her watercolor paints. Also an impulse buy.

She took a breath and looked at the canvas, squinting to blur the sight of the stark white. Her first impulse was to choose the black paint. But the part of her that had slipped the discipline of the past years rebelled. She didn't have to follow Alistair's guidance.

But despite that defiance, her thoughts shifted as she imagined a dark sky with heavy scudding clouds. Then, below that, water. Billowing waves foaming toward the darkened sky.

The darkness that had filled her life after Eli's death now took a different shape. Instead of fighting it, she gave in. Let it wash over her, and as she did, she let her brush dictate what was put on the canvas.

She lost herself in her art, a mixture of exhilaration and discovery feeding her as with stroke after stroke she built up the picture. It was as if her critical mind had been silenced and inspiration overtook her.

But slowly reality seeped into the moment when the canvas was full and she knew she was done.

Stepping back, she took in what she had just created. Her heart leapt in her throat.

How could this have happened?

She had painted a small blue kayak half submerged in the waves of a turbulent sea. She pressed a fist to her mouth. She knew exactly whose kayak it was.

Eli's.

So often she had imagined his last moments, wondering if he'd been afraid. Wondering if fear had choked him.

And always, behind that, the taunting thought that maybe he had survived.

Though her practical mind had told her it wasn't possible, not after all this time, she realized she had held onto that imperceptible hope for years. Had let it linger. Each time she saw someone who even vaguely resembled him, her heart would skip a beat. Once she even called out his name.

And now she looked at the painting, thinking of her brother, thinking of happier times. Of the comfort he had given her. When her teenage heart was broken. Whenever she and Annie would have a fight. When she had to deal with her first critique of her work. When she grieved the loss of their mother. He knew how she felt. He understood her every emotion. They were that connected.

She pulled in a quivering breath.

The empty kayak. Her brother, gone.

And somehow, deep within her, she knew Eli was at peace.

With shaking hands, she picked up a brush, watered down some yellow paint, blended in a hint of brown, and gently added one last touch. A gentle ray of sunshine breaking through the roiling clouds above and shining just in front of his little boat.

Into the light, she thought with an ironic smile.

Eli had always known who his Savior was. Where his faith and salvation lay. She didn't need to worry about him. She knew that now. She set the brush down and folded her arms over her chest, as if to hold back the grief that was slowly rising.

Her throat thickened with all the unshed tears she had held back all these years. She had never dared to release them because that meant acknowledging her brother really was dead.

A sob clawed its way up her throat. She swallowed it down, but another one followed it. Then another.

The sorrow she had tried to push back all these years made itself known.

She fell to the floor, her arms clutched over her head as if to brace herself.

And she gave in to her heart-wrenching grief.

The light was still on in Etta's cabin.

Finn heard country music coming from inside the cabin and he had to smile. Had he converted her? He waited, listening to one of his favorite country artists singing about open spaces, blue skies, jagged mountain peaks, and deep prairie soil. The song had always resonated deeply with him no matter where he went. He knew, deep down inside, he belonged in this country. He belonged back here, back home.

And now he was falling for a woman who had every intention of moving back to the city.

His brothers used to say he was too impulsive. It was that same impulsiveness that made him walk up the wooden steps to the porch of Etta's cabin. He stood in front of the door, his hand lifted to knock, wondering if he was being smart.

The heart wants what the heart wants.

But was he being smart about this, or selfish?

He was about to turn away when he heard another sound braided through the country music. As the song faded to an end, he cocked his head, listening a little better, and his heart quivered.

Deep sobs barely muffled by the closed door filled the cabin.

Etta.

That was all he needed. He went inside.

Eta sat on the floor, her arms wrapped around her tucked-up legs, her face pressed to her knees.

Sobbing her heart out.

He felt like an intruder, but the sound of her grief tore at his heart. Without stopping to think, he rushed over to her side, dropped on the floor beside her, and pulled her into his arms. She leaned into him, her head tucked under his chin. He stroked her hair away from her damp face and pressed a gentle kiss to the top of her head. Giving her what silent comfort he could.

He didn't know exactly how long they sat there. He held her, thankful for the small encouragement he could give.

Finally, her sobs eased, and she pressed her palms against her eyes.

She swallowed then drew away, digging into her pocket and pulling out a tissue. Finn kept his hand resting on the back of her neck. Words were unnecessary and would get in the way.

"Sorry about that." She wiped her eyes and nose, still looking down.

Finn was about to offer her some assurance when he saw the painting on the easel.

"I'm guessing that's Eli," he said, his hand now making gentle circles on her back.

Etta sniffed again then looked up at the painting as well.

"It is."

That was all she said, but he heard in those two words an expression of six years of pain and longing and grief.

And he realized that while the rest of the painting was done in her signature shades of black, gray, and white, the kayak was a bright blue and the ray of light was painted in a watery yellow. The only colors on the entire canvas.

Etta blinked, wiping at her face again, then slowly got to her feet. "Blue was his favorite color."

Finn stayed beside her, both of them looking at the painting.

"I don't know what came over me. I just started painting," she said, her voice uneven.

He moved a step back to see it better. "I wish I knew more about art so I could make some profound statement. I just know it's very moving. A very powerful painting."

Though he wished she had put more color in it, he also recognized the work for what it was. A small step in another direction.

And that's when he saw the other painting resting against the wall.

"Did you just do that?" he asked, moving closer to examine it more carefully. A vague outline of a cowboy superimposed over a mountain landscape.

"Oh...that's just something I was experimenting with. Just playing around. Nothing really." She sounded apologetic, and he wondered why.

"That's where I took you," he said, a sense of wonder entering his voice. "And you even did it in color."

"I was just fooling around. Trying to get inspired."

"And it looks like our little nature trip helped out." He looked closer at the cowboy. "Is that...me?"

She said nothing to that and he wondered if he had pushed things too far. But when he looked back at her, she had her arms crossed over her chest, a faint smile edging her lips. "Yes. It is. I figured I may as well pay homage to the man who helped me break through my painter's block."

"Is that a thing?"

"Is now."

"Interesting that you did this one in color," he said, pointing to the painting beside him, "and that one in mostly black and white." Other than the kayak and the ray of sun.

Etta bit her lip, glancing from the painting of Finn to the one of Eli as if comparing them.

"I think the one of Eli is closer to what I used to paint. After Eli...went missing...I was in a dark and uncertain place, and black and white seemed to be the only way I could express myself. When I started art school out of college, I met a man—professor—who became a...a type of, well..." Her voice faded away and her arms clasped even tighter around her midsection.

"Became a type of..." Finn prodded, wondering at her hesitation.

"He became like a mentor," Etta finally said. "He told me anyone can paint color. Black and white was my forte, and that was what he guided me to do. So I kept painting monochrome. It fit where I was at emotionally at the time."

"And now?"

"Now I don't know what kind of artist I am." She looked over at the painting of Finn and sighed again. "I had a lot of fun painting that one."

"Why don't you paint more like that?"

"I don't know."

She sounded so despondent that Finn couldn't stay where he was. He walked over, took her by the arm, and led her to the couch.

"What don't you know?" he asked, feeling as if there was still something else she wanted to say. Something else to tease out.

"Painting the one of you was easy and the one of Eli, hard," she said, looking as if someone had kicked her in the stomach.

Which, given what she had just gone through, didn't surprise him.

He went out on a limb. "Did you cry after Eli...after Eli died?"

Etta kneaded her hands, staring straight ahead. Then she released a harsh laugh. "I didn't know when I could. At what moment could I decide he was gone? When could I say, 'now I can grieve his loss'?"

Her simple answer tore at his heart. Of course. If there is no body how does one acknowledge the passing?

"This is the first time?"

She nodded. He slipped his arm around her shoulders and pulled her close, giving her what comfort he could. "I'm so sorry to hear that," he said, laying his cheek on her head, holding her with both arms. He felt he'd been given a glimpse of an intimate part of her soul. And he was thankful he could be here for her now.

She released a heavy sigh and nestled closer.

They stayed that way a long time, and while he held her, he looked from the painting of Eli to the one of himself, trying not to read too much into the situation.

However, he couldn't ignore the symbolism inherent in each painting. One so full of life and color, the other an expression of deep pain with a glimmer of hope.

Dear Lord, help me give this hurting woman what she needs, Finn prayed, stroking her head with his cheek.

He didn't know where things were going, but for now he was willing to go along for the ride.

CHAPTER NINE

*E*tta's phone rang as she turned on the coffeemaker. She glanced at the screen and debated whether she should talk to her sister.

But last night had been a tumbling whirlpool of emotions. And not all of them to do with her tears over Eli.

"Hey you," she said as she pulled out a mug and sugar.

"Hey yourself. How's things going since we last talked?" Annie's voice sounded tinny, which meant she was probably talking on her Bluetooth connection on her way to work. Which meant they had about three-quarters of an hour.

"Um, all over the place. What about you?"

"Work is going good. I'm going on my second date with Murphy, so that's a plus."

"Is that the hot date you told me about on Saturday?"

"Yes."

"You sound excited."

"Life is good these days. So, talk to me about the cowboy."

Etta's gaze slid over to the paintings. After Finn left last night, she had taken Eli's painting off the easel and set it beside the one of Finn. Eli's was larger, but the one of Finn drew her eye each time.

And despite her grief, made her smile.

"I cried in his arms last night."

"Okay?" Annie sounded like she wasn't sure what to make of that.

"I painted a picture of Eli." Her voice choked up as remnants of last night's emotions seeped into today.

"Wow. Can you send me a picture later?"

"Of course." She poured herself a cup of coffee then turned, studying the paintings again.

"Was that why you cried in the cowboy's embrace? Hmm. That sounds like the name of a romance novel."

"Be a suitable name for a painting I made of him," Etta returned.

"Painting? Oh my. I'll get to that later. Tell me about the tears. Were they because of Eli?"

"Yes."

In the moment of silence that followed her reply, Etta heard the sounds of the city. Cars honking, a siren sounding in the distance. She felt like it had been years since she was in the same place Annie was now instead of six weeks.

Battling traffic, trying to get to school on time. Fighting a sense of panic as the clock moved faster than the car ahead of her.

To her surprise, she found she didn't miss it.

"You haven't cried since we got the news. At least not that I know of."

"You're right. But somehow, being here, being with Finn—" She stopped herself before she could say anything more. "Being in this incredible country. I feel like it's opened up parts of my life I've been keeping closed down."

"Parts of your life Alistair kept closed down as well," Annie said.

"Maybe."

"No. For sure. He had his own idea of what you should paint, and he pushed you relentlessly. He had way too much control over your life." Annie's voice took on the usual snark it got when she talked about Alistair.

"It was my signature style," Etta said by way of a feeble defense, not wanting to think Alistair had that much influence over her.

"Only because he shoved you in that direction. I know how hard it's been for you the past few years. You've complained about how difficult it's been to get inspired. I think he pushed you into a smaller and smaller box. He's got a lot to answer for. But enough about him. Has Renate tried to contact you again?"

"No. Thank goodness."

"Now let's discuss the painting you said you might name The Cowboy's Embrace."

Trust Annie to circle back to that.

"It's of Finn." May as well come right out and admit it. Annie would finagle it out of her. She had a knack for that. "When we went out into the mountains."

"Is it colorful?"

"Yes."

"You sound like that's not a good thing."

"I enjoyed painting it. It was invigorating."

"So, paint more pieces like that. I've been pushing you to put more color in your painting for a long time now."

"But my application is based on the pieces I've been doing. Monochrome."

"Pieces that have been becoming more impossible to carry on with. Even Van Gogh moved on from his black-and-white period to more color. And he was depressed most of his life."

"I can't believe you listened to my art school ramblings."

"Honey, I absorbed it all. I'm saying you're allowed to move on. If this painting you did of Eli and of the hunky cowboy inspired you, then move in that direction."

"But my artist-in-residence application was based on my monochrome work."

"Most of which you don't have anymore because of the fire."

Trust Annie to put things in harsh perspective.

"They're getting restored."

"That may be. But I think you should paint from your heart," Annie continued. "Wherever your heart is now. If you apply for that position based on work you don't enjoy doing anymore, you won't be much good as an inspiring teacher then either, will you?"

Etta had to laugh but also sensed the wisdom in what her sister was saying. "I guess you're right," she admitted. "How did you end up so perceptive?"

"Hours of counseling and Netflix." She spoke the words lightly, but Etta knew that beneath her confidence and sharp humor, Annie had her own struggles and demons to wrestle. "So how much inspiration came from this cowboy?"

Etta took a sip of her cooling coffee and moved to the small table and sat down. Still looking at the paintings. The more she looked at them, the more they spoke to her. Two men. Past pain. Future hope?

"The trip we took up into the mountains definitely filled my creative well," she said.

"You cried in his arms. You can't tell me you didn't kiss him somewhere along the way."

"Not last night."

"But another time."

"Yes."

"So. How do you feel about him?"

"I don't know what to feel. Don't know what to think. I'm attracted to him. He's funny and caring and kind."

"I like him already."

"But he's so rooted here. He'd never move to the city."

"Which is where you're headed." Annie's sigh underlined Etta's dilemma. "I see what you're struggling with. But I'm telling you straight up, girl. A career is fine, and it can be satisfying and fulfilling. But there have been many, many times I wish I hadn't walked away from Tim."

When Annie was twenty-one, she dated a young man who wanted to be a large-animal vet. But that would have meant moving to the country, and Annie had her heart set on an internship with a graphics company. They broke up, and she'd never truly got over him from the sounds of it.

"I'm sorry you have to deal with that," Etta said, biting her lip, suddenly uncertain. "But I feel like things are more complicated with Finn and with me."

"And we're back to Alistair and your unfounded guilt."

"Not entirely unfounded."

"Unfounded. Does Finn know about Alistair?"

"We're hardly at the sharing past histories part," she protested.

"Sounds like you might get there."

"Maybe."

"Meantime, ride this wave of inspiration. Paint up a bunch of pictures and see what comes. Send them off to the program coordinator. You might be surprised by what they say. You always tell me how much I should trust God to guide my decisions and my life, maybe it's time to take your own advice. Trust that God put you in this place and space and gave you a unique kind of inspiration. Don't waste this chance. Use it."

As her sister spoke, Etta felt a loosening of the bonds that had gripped her so tightly the past few months. At the same time, she felt a tiny flicker of shame that it was her sister, who had turned her back on God, who was giving her spiritual guidance.

"Thanks for everything," Etta said, smiling. "You're the best sister ever."

"Yeah, I am."

"Love you. And you know, I pray for you too."

"I know. And I'm glad you do."

Annie said good-bye and Etta set her phone on the table, sipping her coffee, looking at the paintings.

But despite her tears and anguish of last night, it was the one of Finn that captured her attention.

Finn knocked on Etta's cabin door Friday morning, his heart lifting a little when he heard her footsteps inside. She opened it and her smile made his heart skip again. He hadn't seen her since Wednesday night. He'd been busy yesterday, and he suspected she was painting. He and Reuben had to go pick up some feed in town so they'd joined Katrina at Coffee on the Corner, Janie Corbett's shop.

This morning he had to check on a couple of late calving cows and then trim horses' hooves.

He was eager to see her again. Hoped maybe he could give her a lift to the fair.

She wore a pink tank top and white skirt. Sandals. Her hair was tied in a sloppy topknot and she had a canvas bag slung over her shoulder. She looked exactly like the artist she was.

"Hey. How's it going?" Oh boy. Finn wanted to do a facepalm but decided not to draw attention to his lame opening. So he just grinned.

"It's going well," she said, looking a bit puzzled. As if wondering why he was here.

"I have a couple of things." He handed her a check. "This is technically from the insurance company."

Etta looked down at the check, frowning. "It's written on the ranch's account."

"That's because the insurance payout on the contents went to the ranch. We are the ones on the policy. Reuben gave me this check this morning."

"This seems like a lot."

"You lost a lot. They also told Reuben that they would settle with the art restorers so you don't have to deal with them either."

Etta blew out a sigh, waving the check and smiling. "This will help. I'll be needing more supplies soon."

"Excellent. But I had another reason for stopping. I'm wondering if you want to ride to the fair with me?"

She glanced past him to her car, parked by the cabin, her smiling growing. "That would be nice. I was just headed out, but I guess there's no sense taking two vehicles."

"I know you want to be back on time to do some work, so we won't be dawdling."

"I had a productive morning. I don't know if I need to rush back."

"Really? That's great." He wanted to ask her how she'd been sleeping. If she was still okay.

And he kind of wanted to see what she'd been painting but thought that would be too pushy.

He also wanted to kiss her and figured that fell into the same category.

Last night he lay in bed awake far too long trying to figure out the way forward with Etta. He knew something was building between them. Something different from what he and Helen had shared. Deeper. Stronger. He pushed down the fact that she was leaving. He knew he wanted to pursue this relationship. See where it would go.

See if he would make sacrifices for it.

"Let's go then," he said, stepping aside for her.

She held up the check. "Just let me put this in the house so I don't lose it."

She went inside and returned quickly, closed the door of the cabin, hesitated, then laughed as she looked back at him. "Sorry. I'm still getting used to not having to lock my door."

"You probably should. The twins are very nosy."

"They've not come around at all," she said as they walked down the wooden steps toward his truck.

"That's because Wyatt put the kibosh on that right away. Made it pretty clear they had to give you your space. Ruby, the nanny, also makes sure they keep their distance."

He opened the passenger door of the truck for her, then offered his hand to help her up.

And she took it. He gave it an extra squeeze as she got in. She returned it with one of her own.

Things are looking good, he thought, whistling as he walked around the front of the truck.

Soon they were on the road, country music playing on the radio.

"I like this song," Etta said.

"You know it?"

She gave him a mischievous grin. "My sister set up a country playlist on my phone. Told me I had to embrace the vibe. I was playing it the other night when…" Her voice tapered off, and Finn shot her a quick glance, knowing she was talking about Wednesday night.

"Hey. How are you doing today?" he asked, reaching across and taking her hand in his.

"I'm doing much better." She looked away, her expression growing solemn. "The last couple of nights were the first time I didn't dream about my brother in years."

"You dreamt about him every night?"

"Not always bad dreams, sometimes just unsettling. But I think doing the painting and…well…talking to you…" She glanced sidelong at him, giving him a wry smile. "Crying with you, let's be honest, I think helped me lay him to rest. Helped me accept that he's gone."

Finn tightened his grip on her hand. "I'm glad I could be there for you."

"Me too." She held his gaze and Finn felt himself getting lost in her eyes. Then corrected as the truck drifted toward the ditch.

"You're too much of a distraction," he said with a good-natured grumble.

"Hey, you're the one who asked me to come with you," she returned.

He laughed and once again felt that wonderful and welcome connection with her.

Yes, he was willing to see where things went.

❧ · ☙

Etta's pencil flew over the sketchpad as she glanced up at the little girl sitting in front of her with her hands clasped on her lap then back to the paper. A smile crawled across her face as a little girl's features slowly took shape. As she worked, she was reminded of that first year in art school when she did numerous sketches.

And once again, the old enthusiasm for drawing returned. She felt a rush translating what she saw onto paper and adding her own dimension.

While she worked, she tried to block out the people gathered around her, watching. She heard their surprised comments, their compliments. The little girl's mother was encouraging her daughter to sit still. That didn't really matter to Etta. She was capturing the essence of the child, not portraying her exactly. A few more smudges, a few more pencil strokes. She had to catch herself from going overboard. From overworking the piece. Something her art teacher had often chastised her about.

"When it's done, it's done," she could hear Mrs. Doritsky saying in her head.

She loved that art teacher. That was before Alistair.

She slammed the door on that thought, then carefully pulled the sketch off the pad and handed it to the little girl's mother.

"Thank you," the woman said, her voice holding a tinge of amazement as she looked at the sketch. "This is fantastic. How did you manage to capture her so easily and so quickly?"

"It's because she's an amazing artist," Finn said, which made Etta blush. She gave him a look of reprimand.

Which didn't even register on the guy. Though he had come and gone, for the most part he stayed here. Watching her. It should have bothered her, but she gained some small comfort from his support.

"My turn, my turn," a couple of kids called out.

"You'll get your turn," Adele said. She was standing by the table where people had signed up. She looked down at her clipboard and called out another name.

This time it was a little boy and his older sister. The mother fussed with the kids and the father encouraged them to sit still. Etta sharpened her pencils, took a moment to study the children, and went to work again.

Joy suffused her as she worked, capturing these two little kids. When she was done their parents also expressed their admiration.

Seriously, if anything this exercise was the self-esteem boost any artist needed. Their praise was like candy.

The next few were adults, which created a bit more pressure. Adults tended to be more guarded and less enthused about how they were captured.

But she did her best, and from the exclamations of awe and excitement, she felt she had succeeded.

She wasn't even sure how many she'd done. Time had become meaningless. Each person was a new challenge, and she felt more alive than she had in years.

Then she felt Finn's hand on her shoulder.

"Adele said you need to take a break and I have to agree," he said.

Etta blinked, pulling herself back into the moment, and looked around.

The crowd, obviously spread by word-of-mouth, had gotten even bigger. Etta tried not to feel the pressure of all the people who wanted to have her capture their portrait.

"I can go for a little while longer," she said.

"Maybe, but I want to take you around the fairgrounds. You look like a woman in need of mini donuts."

Etta clutched her pencil, glancing from the crowd to Finn and then over to Adele, who was nodding.

"We can put your names down in order of how you are currently lined up," Adele announced. "Just come back at three and you can get your sketch done by our own Etta Caprice."

Our own. Like she was some long-lost hometown girl who had made her way back to Millars Crossing.

"Okay. Let's go," Finn said, holding his hand out to Etta to help her up. She didn't need the assistance but she took it anyway, feeling that tiny thrill again as his work-roughened hand clasped hers.

"Unfortunately, this is just a small-town fair," Finn said as he led her through the people ambling down the grass fairway, still holding her hand. "So we don't have the massive Ferris wheel we can go up on and I can bribe the guy to stop when we're at the top so I can kiss you."

"I'm glad they don't have a Ferris wheel," she said with a shudder.

"What? You don't want me to kiss you?"

She did, actually, very much. He'd been on her mind a lot the past few days. He made her not want to think too much about the future. Just be in the here and now, something she wasn't used to. She liked planning. She liked control.

This was different.

"I'm terrified of Ferris wheels. I went on one once with Eli. It wasn't even a big one, but we got stuck at the top and he rocked the seat back and forth. I tried to tell myself we'd be okay, but it didn't work. I hated that feeling of being suspended and nothing under me. I couldn't wait to get off. Haven't been on one since."

"I wouldn't rock your seat," Finn assured her, squeezing her hand just a bit tighter. "But I would hope I would rock your world if I kissed you."

"Oh. No. Please, I can't believe you just said that," Etta said with a laughing groan.

"It was right there. Waiting for me to say it," Finn returned, laughing as well.

"Where are we headed?" she asked, stepping aside to let a couple with a baby stroller pass by them.

"I told you. Mini donuts. We'll take them to the river and sit on the bench and eat them. I might even let you have one."

"So generous."

"That's me. Heart of gold."

She had to laugh, surprised again at how easy he was to be around. How quickly she felt this comfortable with him.

And after Wednesday night, she felt connected to him in a way she had never felt with anyone else. She thought today would be awkward, but as soon as she saw him on her doorstep it just felt right.

"Major score," Finn said, pulling her along to the mini doughnut van. "No line." He put in his order and when it was ready, took the greasy paper bag, grinning like a little kid.

"You sharing those?" a tall dark-haired man behind them asked him.

"Not with you, Logan. You'd eat them all, lick your fingers, and ask me if I can get you more."

The man named Logan just laughed, then glanced over at Etta. "I saw you in church, but I don't think we've ever been introduced. I'm Logan Carleton."

His angular features and stubbled chin created a bad-boy vibe emphasized by the cowboy hat.

"You gotta watch out for this guy," Finn said, shifting as if coming between her and Logan. "He's a love 'em and leave 'em kind of guy."

Logan released a bark of laughter. "That's your schtick, mister, not mine."

"You still haven't forgiven me for my crush on Sarah, have you," Finn teased.

"That was years ago," Logan said, his smile taking on an edge. "I think I've gotten over it."

"I'm sure you have. How's business been?"

"Challenging, but good. Things are looking up."

"That's good. But I better get moving so you can order yours."

"They're not for me. Billy put in his order."

"You're such a good brother," Finn said with another grin. "I doubt I would do the same for Reuben or Wyatt. But I got a hot date with some donuts and with this lovely lady." He angled his head toward Etta.

"In that order?" Etta teased.

"Priorities," he returned, taking her arm. "See you around," he said to Logan, pulling Etta along. He put his head closer to hers. "Don't get all caught up in that dark, brooding look that my cousin, Logan has perfected. Deep down he's a bundled mass of insecurities."

"Heard that," Logan called out, but Etta could see he was chuckling.

As they walked toward the river, Finn said hi to a few more

people. Some of them Etta remembered from church. A Mrs. Flikkema who had introduced herself to Etta as the owner of an Airbnb. A woman named Trix, and the owner of the local pizza place she had visited from time to time, Cal Chernowsky.

Finn stopped to chat with Cal briefly, telling him that he was glad he had put the meat lovers special back on the menu.

Cal chuckled and said he had done it because he heard Finn was back in town.

"He's a great guy and makes great pizza," Finn commented as they walked away.

"I know. Other than the meal I had at the ranch house, I've eaten his pizza every Saturday since I've come here."

"Just Saturdays?" Finn asked as they walked down a narrow path toward the river. "I think if I was on my own, I'd be eating there twice a day."

"Even breakfast?"

"Especially breakfast."

"I'd have those mini donuts for breakfast before pizza," Etta said with a chuckle. "Unless they're just for you."

Finn looked shocked and pulled his bag closer to himself in a defensive gesture. "You didn't buy your own bag?"

Again, Etta had to laugh.

"Lucky for you, I'm a generous guy," he said, then pointed to a bench a few feet off the trail. "I thought we could sit here and eat and, just to give you a sneak peek, I'll give you one right now." He held out the bag for her, and she took two.

"What is that?" he asked in mock horror.

"It's me taking two donuts."

As he lowered himself onto the bench, he shook his head as if he couldn't believe what had just happened. "That's pretty audacious."

"Live for the moment, because you never know when you'll have mini donuts again," she returned.

He laughed at that but then held the bag out to her. "Take as many as you want. I'm nothing if not forgiving."

She chuckled and settled back against the bench, sitting close to Finn but not too close. They had shared many moments together but she didn't want to presume. Not yet.

"How's the artist stuff going?" he asked, wiping his sugary hands on one of the napkins he had tucked into the bag.

"The paintings? Quite well, actually."

"Color, or shades of gray?"

"I have some amazing portraits of horses, mountains, and flowers I think would suit you." While she was teasing, she did have a few canvases she was happy with. Watercolors of ghostly flowers overlaid over mountain scenes. It had been easier to experiment in that medium because all of her previous work had been in oil. This felt like a complete break from her old work.

And it had been surprisingly freeing.

"I'll have to check them out," he said, holding the bag out to her to take another donut. She took two again, just to tease him, but this time he didn't say anything.

They sat together, quiet, listening to the water splashing past them. It was soothing and Etta wished she had brought her sketchpad so she could capture the water flowing over the rocks, the way the sun sprinkled flickers of light dancing off the waves, the trees just beyond them protecting the river, and the glimpse of the mountains through the trees.

"This is such a beautiful place," she said, brushing the sugar off her fingers. Finn handed her a napkin and she took it with a shy smile.

"You like it here?"

"I do. It fills my artist soul."

"Think you could live here?"

He spoke the question casually, like he had merely tossed it out, but she felt a nip of some unspoken expectation.

"I might, just not sure what I would do. How could I support myself?"

He was silent at that, as if he realized that for himself.

"Would you have to?"

She didn't want to analyze "why" he would ask that question, so she took it at face value. "When my father died, my mother had zero marketable skills. She got work as a grocery store clerk. She barely supported us, there was never enough money for three kids. We all took on part-time jobs while we were in our junior and senior years of high school. There was no shame in it, and it taught me, Annie, and Eli to learn to take care of ourselves. It was an important lesson to me though, not to have limited choices, like my mother did. I know money isn't everything, but she often told us that if we don't build our own dream we'll be hired by people who are living theirs. I don't ever want to be in that position. I want to be able to take care of myself. Live my own dreams."

A beat of silence and then she could see Finn nodding in agreement. "I understand. I'm sure it was hard seeing your mother struggle like that."

"I remember her coming home from working an evening shift and her feet would be swollen and her back sore. She would look at us and tell us that we need to work with this"— she pointed to her head—"and not try to make a living with this." She held her hands out.

"Wise woman."

"She did what she had to, but she pounded into us to be in a position to be able to take care of ourselves regardless of what life threw at us. To make sure we had skills. Make sure we could support ourselves. I've never forgotten those lessons."

"You must miss her."

"Probably as much as you miss your parents."

Finn handed her the bag for her to take the last donut but she waved it off. They were delicious but they were also filling.

"Probably. But you've had much more grief in your life than I have."

Etta nudged aside the memories. She would come to them again sometime. At least now she knew they wouldn't claw as deeply as they once had.

"When will you hear from the university about your application?" Finn asked.

"I have to see if they will accept photos of my work rather than my bringing them in personally."

"If you send photos, would you send them what you've been doing the past few days?"

And wasn't that the question of the hour?

"I'm not sure. It's vastly different from my previous work." She pulled in a long breath and folded her arms over her chest, watching the sun dancing on the waves ahead of them. "I'm scared they would reject it. And then where would I be?"

"Why not present both styles? See what they think? Unless you have to wait to get your paintings back from the restorers."

"I have some pictures I took of them."

"If they'll accept photos, try it and see what happens."

The thought shifted the load in her mind that had been resting there while she worked on the watercolors. It had been frustrating because she had enjoyed this new medium more than she wanted to admit. It was as if letting go of the grief of losing Eli had washed the gray out of her life. And being held by Finn had given her strength and inspiration to go on.

"I'm supposed to present in ten days, so I'm not sure what to do. I'm supposed to come up with ten pieces, and I've only done seven in monochrome. But this morning I did one. In watercolor."

"That's fantastic. That leaves one more to do."

"I'll probably do a few more in color, but at the same time it's hard to stifle the criticism of my professor as I'm working. I keep hearing his advice." She stopped and pressed her lips together, wishing she could put Alistair entirely out of her mind.

"Which is?" Finn prompted.

"That paintings need time to create. To come to fruition. That painting fast is for amateurs."

"Have I heard of this guy? Is he some famous artist?"

The question made her smile. Trust Finn to put things into perspective.

"No, you haven't heard of Alistair."

"Is that the guy who you said was your mentor?" The question was thrown out casually but she heard an underlying wariness. As if he sensed that Alistair was more than a mere mentor.

"Yes. That was him." She stopped again, her heart suddenly racing, choking off her breathing. She felt like her foolishness and indiscretion was written all over her face. She wanted to say more but to what end? She wasn't sure where she and Finn were headed. A few kisses didn't make a relationship.

But she caught that thought, knowing what was happening between them was more than a few kisses. There was an undeniable connection she'd never had with anyone else before.

"He was just a teacher," Finn said.

"Yes. Just a teacher." And she hoped he would move on from anything to do with Alistair.

"That solves that problem. You know the old saying, those that can't do, teach."

"Which is the path I'm hoping to head down," she said, struggling not to feel defensive.

"Sorry, I didn't mean any disrespect." He wiped his hands and folded up the napkins and paper bag. He leaned to one side and slipped them in the back pocket of his jeans. "I better remember that's there or I'll have shredded paper all over my blue jeans when I do laundry again."

"I still can't believe you do your own laundry."

"It's a huge step up from washing it by hand in some tiny sink in a shared bathroom in a hostel."

"What sent you haring around the world?"

He gave her a crooked smile that seemed to hold a note of embarrassment. "A girl who I thought broke my heart and my trust. And that's all I'm saying about that."

His easy dismissal of his previous relationship gave her a small flicker of hope. If he was able to put that aside then maybe she should be able to do the same.

"Let's not delve into the past too much," he said, shifting a little closer then touching her chin. "Right now you've got some sugar there," he said, brushing it off.

They were so close, his face was almost a blur. She didn't know who moved first, but then their lips were touching. Lightly, then closer, and the kiss deepened.

And Etta's heart felt like it had come home.

CHAPTER TEN

"Come have a cup of tea before you go to the barn. Tell me what the lovely Etta is up to these days," Carly said, sitting down at the table in the kitchen with her cup of tea. "I haven't seen her for a while.

Finn glanced at the clock. He had checked on the heifer who was calving just before dinner, but nothing was happening. He had time to join his sister.

"She's been lying low the past few days," he answered, pouring himself a mug of tea. "She's focused on getting her paintings done. I think she's feeling the pressure of her application."

Saturday morning Finn had stopped by Etta's cabin and shared a cup of coffee with her. He had hoped to do more than that, but she was itching to get back to painting. She had several sketches lying around that she had shown him. One was of the river. A few quick studies of people at the fair.

While he would have loved to sit and watch her work, he guessed she didn't want him around.

He had hoped to talk to her on Sunday, but she wasn't in church. Monday he was gone all day with Wyatt to check out some tractors at an upcoming auction. When he got home the light was off in Etta's cabin.

Tonight Wyatt and the kids had gone to town to eat at Adele's apartment. Reuben was helping Katrina clear out the remnants of the plants from the greenhouse. It had been just him and Carly for dinner.

"I heard her sketches were a huge hit at the fair on Friday," Carly said, resting her elbows on the table, taking another sip of her tea.

"Yeah. They were. I had to drag her away because I knew she wanted to get some work done yet that afternoon. And she's been busy since."

"You haven't felt the need to stop by?"

"Oh, I have, but I don't want to bother her." He had been encouraged by their time Friday at the river. By her easy acceptance of his kiss. Things were altering, but the fact that she had retreated to paint was a reminder to him of where she was going. What she wanted to do.

Leave.

"Why don't you ask Etta if she wants to come with you to check on the heifer?"

He held that thought a moment, then shrugged. "Not so sure. She's a city girl. She might find it gross."

"Or interesting," Carly returned.

"Maybe."

Carly set her mug down, holding his gaze. "Tell me. What's happening? Just when I think you two are getting together, you seem to pull apart."

Finn lifted his shoulder in a casual shrug. "I'm not sure."

"Well, how do you feel about her? Last we talked it seemed like you were dithering."

"Still am. Right now she's in her cabin getting the last of her paintings done for that job she's applied for."

"And what if she doesn't get it?"

Finn hadn't thought of that. Wasn't sure what to make of it.

"I'm sure she will. She's super talented."

"And if she left? How would you feel?"

"Lousy." He stared down at the thread of steam rising from his mug and blew on it. "She's such an amazing woman. I feel a connection with her unlike anything I've ever felt before."

"Even with Helen?"

"Absolutely."

"Which means you're kind of stuck then, aren't you?"

His sister's bald statement underlined his own uncertainty. He rubbed his chin and heaved out a sigh. "It seems that way."

"Would you move?"

Another sigh as he tested that thought on for size. Tried to imagine himself living in the city. "I don't know. I was glad to come back here. I'm loving the work, loving being involved in the ranch and working with Reuben and Wyatt. It's home."

"I know. That's why I came back too."

Finn sipped his tea, his thoughts shifting around. What mattered the most to him? "I've always imagined myself living here on the ranch, raising my kids here."

"Lots of people raise happy families in the city," Carly returned.

"I know."

"You just have to figure out what you want more. Which decision would you regret more? It's hard to find someone you're compatible with, especially if you've got history like you and I do. We get fussier. More particular. More set in our ways. But I think you still can change where you're headed."

"And if I go to the city? What about Wyatt and Reuben?" He

couldn't believe he was even saying this, but he felt as if he had to try the concept on. See how it fit him.

"They'd manage. Maybe I'll find some amazing cowboy to marry who wants to live on the ranch. That would help."

"Yeah, cause there's such a huge stash of amazing cowboys around. I think me, Reuben, and Wyatt have the corner on that market."

Carly chuckled. "Yeah, much as I hate to admit it, you guys pretty much fit that bill."

"Why, Sis, I believe that's the kindest thing you've ever said to me."

She flicked her finger at him. "Don't hold me to it. I can just as easily retract that."

"No, words spoken are like arrows. Once released they cannot be returned."

"Wow. Such wisdom. You pick that up in your travels?"

"Nope. Saw it on Facebook." He drank up the last of his tea then took the mug to the counter. "I better go check on that heifer."

"And I better finish up my Netflix series."

"Sounds like we both got a thrilling night ahead of us."

Carly chuckled, then snapped her fingers. "I'm losing my mind," she said. "Reuben sent me a text. He met with the adjuster at the house this afternoon. They're hoping Etta can go to the restorer to check on the paintings on Thursday."

"They're in Calgary, aren't they?"

"Yeah."

Finn went over his week. He and Reuben were going to the auction tomorrow. If they bought the tractor, they would have to pick it up Wednesday.

Thursday Wyatt hoped to cut hay and Finn needed to help. His life was getting busier. Guess Etta would have to go the city on her own. Not that she needed him to drive her, but it would have been a nice time together.

"I'll let her know," he said.

"And ask her to come check the heifer."

Finn chuckled as he stepped outside. The sun was setting. The longest day of the year was a week ago. In another couple of weeks they would cut their first hay and bale it. Getting the feed ready for the winter. It was an endless cycle of keeping animals alive.

And it was where his soul found refreshment. He looked up at the darkening sky. A few stars sparkled back at him. Mars was glowing above the horizon. If he was up early enough in the morning, he'd see Venus.

When he was a kid, his family used to lie out on a blanket and look up at the night sky, looking for the constellations. The Big Dipper or Ursa Major, Ursa Minor, Cassiopeia, Lyra, and others. Could he see the stars as clearly in the city? He doubted it.

Would it matter if he was with Etta?

Were they that far in their relationship?

He shook off the questions and was about to head out to the barn when he saw the door of Etta's cabin open. She stepped outside and he paused, wondering if she could see him in the gathering dusk. He called out to her.

"Hey you. How's it going?"

"Hey yourself. It's going great." She sounded happy, which made him smile. "What are you up to?"

Her question made him change trajectory, and he walked toward her cabin. "I'm checking up on a heifer that's calving."

"I thought most of the cows had already calved."

He was surprised she even knew that. "They have. This one is late, and because she's a first-calver, I want to keep an eye on her."

"Where is she?"

"In the barn." He hesitated, but only for a fraction of a

second as Etta came down the stairs toward him. "Do you want to come?"

"Would that be okay?"

"Of course. I just asked you."

"I mean, with the heifer."

"She'll be fine. She's quiet. Wyatt bottle-fed her as a calf, so she's used to people."

"Okay. Let me get a sweater." She disappeared but came back with not only a sweater but a bag slung over her shoulder. The same bag she'd taken to the fair a few days ago. Probably held her sketchpad.

"Most people take a camera if they want to record things," Finn joked as she joined him.

"I'm old-fashioned," she returned. "Besides, these are the tools of many a court reporter."

"Only because they can't use cameras which, I'm sure, they would sooner do."

"Maybe, but I think you capture different essences when you're sketching. Catch different emotions because you're paying attention with another part of your mind."

"Did I ever tell you how smart you are?"

"No. But you can now."

Though they hadn't had what he wanted to call any kind of meaningful conversation since their shared kiss at the river, he was surprised how easily they fell back into the comfortable give-and-take they shared.

This is rare. This is special.

The words drifted into his mind, then stopped, taking root.

He took a chance and caught her hand, and she wrapped her fingers around his. As if the past few days had been a wisp of smoke blown away by their closeness.

But he couldn't let them go that easily as they walked across the yard, the air cooler now. "You've been busy the past few days," he said, aiming for casual, hoping he hit it.

"I'm so inspired, I didn't want to lose the momentum." He caught her shy upward look at him, and her gentle smile. "I'm sorry if you thought I was neglecting you, but it's been so long since I couldn't stop painting, I didn't want to lose the flow."

"I don't blame you. I felt the same."

"You've been painting too?"

Finn thought of the paints he had bought on a whim, then laughed. "Yes. I've got some amazing etchings I'd like you to check out."

"Yeah, I'm not falling for that corny old line."

"What if it's true?"

"You don't do etchings with watercolors, doofus. You're talking to an expert here."

He laughed, again letting himself just be with her. Enjoying the moment. The hip-roof barn was just up ahead, a watery light shining out from a paned glass window, slanting a small rectangle of gold onto the ground.

"Well, you are coming with me to a barn," he said, angling her a wry look.

"To see a cow calving."

"Heifer."

"Hey, give me a break. I'm still learning."

"Sorry. I shouldn't have corrected you. Bad habit."

They got to the barn and he released her hand and slid open the large wooden door.

"I always wondered what was inside," she said, following him inside and looking at the heavy timbers above.

"We don't use it much, but the kids love playing in here. We have a cat who had kittens, so she's around somewhere."

"It's a beautiful building," she said, turning a slow circle, checking out the horse pens, the ladder to the loft.

"It's a lot of work is what it is," Finn grumbled. "Carly has some idea of incorporating it into her events center. She wants to turn it into a chapel where she can host small weddings."

"This would be an amazing place to have a wedding."

Finn couldn't help the stutter of his heart, thinking of the wedding Helen had been planning. On this property. She too had eyed the barn but mostly as a place to stage wedding pictures.

But right behind that came a measure of relief that he had dodged that particular bullet. He had occasionally wondered what their life might have been like had she not cheated on him, but had always stopped those thoughts. That was a path he did not need to go down.

"You look serious," Etta said, giving him a gentle poke in his side.

"We might be about to witness the birth of a baby calf. Serious business," he said, his smile contradicting his comment.

"I'm sure it is," she said with a mock frown. "Though I have to confess, I've never witnessed this before. I might be squeamish."

"I'm sure you'll be fine. You sketched bunches of kids with popsicle mouths and chocolate on their faces on Friday at the fair. This isn't much different."

"Somehow I doubt that."

He heard the heifer rustling in the straw and as he got nearer the pen, he could see she was lying down, her head extended.

He carefully opened the gate. The heifer didn't move, but her one leg came up and Finn could see the contraction taking hold.

"We came just in time." He pointed to a straw bale. "You can sit there if you want a ringside seat."

"I feel a bit like a voyeur," Etta admitted, but she followed him into the pen and sat down, pulling out her sketchpad. She sat a moment, though, hands folded on the pad, just watching.

"Trust me, she doesn't care."

"How long does it take?"

"The way she's acting, I'm sure it'll be in the next ten or twenty minutes."

"Wow. Impeccable timing on our part."

He liked the way she said *our*. Like they were together.

And wasn't that what was happening? What he hoped they were moving towards?

"Hey, you can see the hooves coming out," he said, pointing.

Etta shifted to see and shook her head in wonder. "Wow. That's cool. A bit gross, but still cool."

"Any minute now."

They were both silent, sitting side by side on the bale, watching. The overhead bulb shed a weak light. Just enough so they could see what was happening and also enough to create soft and intimate shadows.

Etta opened her sketchpad and her pencil flew over the page. He glanced sidelong at it, then turned back to the heifer when she groaned.

"Look, the feet are out, and here comes the head."

A few more pushes and then the miracle occurred.

The calf lay there, wet, complete. For a moment it did nothing. This was the part where Finn always had to make himself wait and see what happened.

The calf lay there another minute but Finn could see it breathing, then it lifted its head, gave it a shake as if to orient itself to this strange and cold world.

"Here comes the best part," Finn said in a hushed whisper.

The mother got her legs under her then lumbered to her feet. She heaved a deep breath, as if thankful the whole procedure was over. Then she turned to her baby and licked it, her rough tongue rasping over the tiny body.

"She's doing that for three reasons," Finn explained, grinning as he watched. "To clean the calf, but she's also bonding with it. The calf shaking its head is a good sign. It's a strong stimulus for the cow to start the licking and connecting. Plus, the cow's tongue is rough, which helps the calf's circulation. It's wet and needs to warm up fast."

Etta had already flipped the page in her sketchpad and was working again. "I thought she was a heifer."

"Well, now that she's had a baby, I guess she's an official cow."

Etta chuckled but kept sketching.

Finn shifted off the bale, knelt down, and moved closer to the calf. He watched the cow, but she paid no attention to him. He carefully reached out to touch the calf.

The cow emitted a low moo, but it seemed less of a threat and more of a gentle warning.

The calf shook its head again and then struggled to get up on its own. Bull calf, from what Finn could see.

He dropped and tried again, his legs wobbling dangerously as he finally stood.

"This is incredible." Etta's quiet voice took on a note of awe. She still held her pencil, but her hands were motionless as she watched the calf teeter over to its mother. The cow was lowing her encouragement in rumbling tones.

Etta's amazement echoed his own. Didn't matter how often this happened, it was always a miracle.

"Just a few minutes ago there was only one, now there's two," she said. "I know the calf was inside her all the time, but still..." Her voice trailed off as she stared at the damp calf.

"Look. It's trying to find the udder," Finn said, shifting so he could see better.

The calf bumped the cow's belly with its head, emitting a weak bleat. Then tried again, his legs still shaky. The cow turned her head toward him, standing still, nudging him just a little. He took a few staggering steps back then moved in again, nosing the cow's udder. Then, finally, he latched on, sucking greedily.

"There you go, little guy," Finn murmured in approval, settling back on his haunches, content to watch.

The calf drank for a while, sucking noisily, then butted the cow and drank again.

"How do they know what to do?" Etta asked, entranced. "It's incredible."

"It is every time I see it," Finn agreed.

The calf drank some more then pulled back, stumbled to the head of the cow, and dropped down. He curled his legs up under him, and the cow started licking him again.

"I'll get her a drink of water and some feed," Finn said, getting to his feet.

Etta nodded, still watching the calf, but she had flipped another page in her sketchpad and her pencil was dancing again.

Smiling at the sight, he turned and walked to the far end of the barn where they had a tap installed. A few pails lay scattered, and he filled one up and dragged it back to the pen. He set it in a corner so the cow could access it then went back to get some hay from a broken hay bale tucked in another corner.

He set the hay down by the water, which the cow was already slurping down.

"She went there as soon as you left," Etta said, looking up from her sketchpad.

"The new mommas are always thirsty after they give birth. Giving them water right away also helps get the milk production going."

He sat down beside Etta and glanced at her sketchpad, once again amazed at how she had captured the moment with simple strokes of her pencil. Not detailed and yet perfect.

"Do you do much sketching?"

"Mostly for preliminary artwork, but not as much as I used to."

"You have a real gift for it," he said, looking up from the sketchpad. "The people of Millars Crossing seem to think so too."

Etta tapped the top of her pencil against the pad, her expression pensive. "I've always enjoyed it."

"It's a good combination of your talent and your propensity for monochrome."

She shot him a teasing look. "Propensity? Was that the word of the day on your phone?"

He thumped himself on the chest with a fist. "Me Finn. Finn smart," he returned.

Her burst of laughter made him want to hug her. So he did, and she slipped easily into his embrace.

He brushed a kiss over her forehead, a feeling of utter contentment slipping through him. She set her pad and pencil aside, tucked her head under his and snuggled closer, her arm slipping around his waist, her other hand on his knee.

This was a moment he wanted time to stop. Stay right here. Tomorrow would bring its own struggles and questions. Right here, right now, his heart, mind, and soul were at rest.

He didn't know how long they sat there, watching as the cow lowered herself to the straw-covered floor, the calf lying tucked up against her large body. Peace filled the moment.

But slowly, like an unwelcome snake, other thoughts slipped in. Other truths.

"I imagine you've been painting."

"I got three more pieces done."

"Are you happy with them?"

"They're different from my other work, but yes, I am."

"Speaking of other work, Reuben got a call from the company restoring your paintings. They want you to come and have a look at them. Make sure they're up to snuff, I guess."

Etta was quiet, simply sitting beside him. He wondered what was going through her mind right now.

"Okay. I have to make a trip to Calgary soon anyway. I didn't buy near enough watercolor supplies."

"Didn't figure on using them much?"

"Nope. Got lots of gray, black, and white oils, though."

Talk of her paintings brought the future into the moment. He wanted to let it go, but the more time they spent together, the more he wanted to spend together.

But was it fair of him to expect anything of her?

Then what are you doing with her now?

The question slithered into his conscious thoughts as he brushed another kiss over Etta's forehead.

And when she lifted her face to his, their lips touching, mouths moving over each other, arms holding each other close, he pushed the question down into the nether reaches of his thoughts.

Etta closed the door of the cabin on the outside world then leaned against it, clutching her sketchpad, her mind a whirl of emotions and thoughts.

She smiled as she thought of what she had just witnessed. A miracle.

She pushed herself away from the door and walked over to the small table in what served as a dining room and sat. As she flipped through her sketchpad, she felt as if she were reliving the evening.

The last sketch was of Finn, kneeling down, touching the baby calf, a look of wonder on his face.

She hadn't done him justice but was happy with what she had captured. A man so at one with the place he was, that she couldn't imagine him anywhere else.

And she was jealous of that. The last time she had experienced that sense of belonging was before her mother went into the hospital. Despite the difficulties they faced, they were a family. Together.

Just like Finn with his family.

You could have this too.

The thought landed as lightly as a feather, settling in.

She and Finn were growing serious. Connecting more each time they were together. Though she and Alistair had dated for five years, she never felt the same sense of belonging that she had with Finn.

Sometimes you just know.

She looked over at the canvases she had finished, smiling at the sight of the abundance of color and light beaming back at her.

Commonplace. Treacly.

Things Alistair would say whenever he saw artwork that Etta thought of as more accessible and pleasing to the eye than most of the pieces they studied in his class.

She gave the words a moment's attention then, with a short laugh, dismissed them. What did Alistair know of true emotion? He knew nothing about faithfulness and love.

She thought of the time she spent with Finn. How caring he was. How loving with her and with his family.

He was a man whose opinions she should pay attention to.

And right then her phone rang.

Annie.

"Hey you," Etta said.

"I'm stuck in traffic and thought I would check in."

"This time of night?"

"Put in a bunch of extra time on a project I'm working on, and there's construction on the Lion's Gate Bridge."

"There's always construction on the Lion's Gate Bridge," Etta returned.

"Have you heard anything from the university?"

Etta thought of the e-mail she received that afternoon.

"Yes. Once I explained what happened they said they're willing to let me send in photos of my work rather than come in and present the actual pieces themselves. Apparently one of the adjudicators had already seen my work in person and was willing to advocate for me."

"That's great."

"Yeah. It is."

"You don't sound too thrilled."

Etta swallowed the unexpected and unwelcome emotions. She dropped onto the couch, kicked off her sandals, and stretched her legs out, getting comfortable.

"I'm feeling confused."

"About the job, or about the cowboy?"

This made her chuckle, which, she supposed, was Annie's way of dialing down the emotion.

"Both. Wondering where I'm going with my life."

"So, what's the deal?" Annie asked. "Tell big sister what's going on."

"I feel like all I've been doing is dumping on you, and it's not fair."

"Hey, that's how it goes. I'll have my turn someday once you're all settled into your life."

Etta sighed. "And that's the problem. I used to know where I wanted to be settled, but now, I'm not sure. I thought I was on the right path…" Her voice faded away as confusion and second thoughts whirled through her mind.

"Are your questions in any way connected to said cowboy?"

Another sigh bought her a bit more time. "Yeah. I think I'm falling for this guy. This evening I sat with him watching a cow calve, and I saw such a gentle and caring part of him that made me melt."

"I don't blame you. That pic you sent of him up on the mountain was pretty swoon worthy."

"He's such a great guy, and he's making me rethink my plans, but I've let my life be run by a man before, and I don't want that to happen again."

"Can you trust him?"

That was an interesting question. Etta had to ponder on it. Then she nodded. "Yes. I can."

"Then take it one step at a time."

"That sounds good in theory, but what does it look like? I already feel like I've taken a lot of steps that I can't backtrack from." Etta stood up, restless now.

"What's holding you back from committing to him?"

"The job I'm applying for."

"Do you still want it?"

"I don't know."

"You know, I never wanted to say anything before, because you seemed pretty set on this job, but your uncertainty gives me an opening to ask you. Do you really want to be a teacher? Or do you want to be an artist?"

Her sister's question was like a splash of reality, and Etta felt as if, with those questions, Annie had shifted her entire perspective.

"It's just, I can't see you in front of a classroom," Annie said. "I know you used to grumble about having to take over for...for Alistair."

"That was because I didn't always like the direction he would push the students in."

"Maybe, but I also got a sense that you didn't always enjoy it."

Etta sighed, the truth of her sister's comment undermining everything she'd been working toward. And yet, the fact that it could show Etta how flimsy her plans were. "Okay, but what alternative do I have?"

"I think you have to be careful not to think too far ahead. You've spent your whole life doing that."

Annie was right. When Etta was in junior high, all she could think about was which courses she wanted to take in high school. Then, when she was in high school, her focus was on which college to go to. Then it was what to major in. Always looking and planning ahead. When she met Alistair, it was what kind of future they would have and what that would look like.

"I know. It's a struggle to stay in the moment and it's kind of scary."

"Why is it scary?"

"What would I do if I stayed here? How would I support myself?"

"Sell your paintings."

"It's not that easy."

"Actually, it can be. I know you. If you want something, you'll make it work."

Her sister's affirmation erased some tension.

"If I get offered the job, what do I do?"

"Decide then." Etta heard her sister honk her horn. "Sorry. Moron cut me off. Anyway, it sounds to me like there's something else bugging you. Something you're not talking about."

She was right, as usual. No one knew her like her sister did. May as well come right out with it.

"My relationship with Alistair is bugging me. What I did and the repercussions."

"Honey, you have to stop thinking about him and what happened," Annie said, her tone gentle and caring. "You had nothing to do with his marriage breaking up. Nothing. You always tell me you believe God has forgiven you. Maybe you better take that on as truth for yourself."

Etta knew she was right, it just seemed harder to do than it should be. She thought of that moment in church when the pastor talked about forgiveness. Sometimes it was easier to give than receive.

"Have you talked to Finn about Alistair?"

"There's been no reason to tell him. I feel like things have been shifting and changing between us, and I'm still trying to find my balance. I don't know when the time is right to divulge past indiscretions."

"I can see that, but if you are getting serious about this guy, you'll have to tell him. You can't have secrets."

"I know." Despite the progress she had made in her view of Alistair and their relationship, it was still hard to imagine herself laying it out in front of Finn.

"Sounds like you'll be doing a lot of praying the next few days," Annie said.

"I will be," Etta agreed.

They exchanged a few more pleasantries and then said good-bye.

After her sister hung up, Etta lay back on the couch, staring up at the ceiling and wondering which prayer to send up first.

CHAPTER ELEVEN

"How's the hay crop looking?" Etta asked, taking a sip of her iced tea and pushing her swing with one foot.

It was late Thursday evening, and she had just come back from the city, thankful for the peace that now surrounded her. Her ears still rang from the hum of her vehicle and the busyness of driving through city traffic, making decisions and consulting her phone's GPS for directions. When Finn had driven her, it had been much better. Navigating on her own, not so much.

It helped that she had such good company then, as she did now.

Finn sat on a chair on Etta's porch, drinking iced tea, his cowboy hat pushed back on his head. His face was flushed and his shirt sleeves rolled up. The past few days he'd been busy haying and she'd been busy painting. After her conversation with her sister, she felt a need to retreat. To find her balance.

Finn hadn't had time to notice.

He'd been up early each morning and working until late,

cutting hay and, at one time, fixing a tractor. Taking out time for the auction.

She'd had dinner with the family only once, on Wednesday, but it felt awkward without Finn there. The kids were a welcome distraction. Today she wasn't back until well after dinner so she didn't have to turn down yet another invitation from Carly.

Once she had put everything away, she sat outside and just let herself enjoy the quiet.

When he saw her, Finn had come and joined her, and as soon as he did, she felt as if life was exactly how it should be. Crazy how quickly she felt comfortable with this man. How quickly he made her rethink her career path.

"Hay crop is looking good," Finn was saying. "Wyatt figures it's one of our best in a while, which is great considering we'll be expanding our herd."

"And now, after Monday, you have one more calf," she said, giving her swing another push.

"Yup. Should be the last one."

She eased out a gentle sigh, thinking of the sketches and paintings she'd made of the calf.

And of Finn.

She hadn't been able to resist capturing him as he knelt by the baby calf, touching it, a gentle smile on his face. It was almost a cliché moment, but because it was Finn, the sight held a lovely resonance.

Yesterday she had done a painting of that sketch. It was simple, but it spoke to her and, she thought, showed who Finn was.

"And how was Calgary?" he asked.

"Hectic." She blew out a sigh, shaking her head. "I've only been out here a few months, but I can't believe how quickly I've gotten used to quieter roads and smaller stores. I was glad to be back home." She almost corrected herself after saying *home* but figured it would only draw more attention to her verbal slip.

"Where all did you go?"

"The art restorers to check on the progress they were making with the paintings."

"How do they look?"

"Really good. I was impressed. But they were way on the north end of the city. The traffic was nuts. Made me even happier you drove the last time we went. I had to avoid construction to get downtown to the art supply store."

And thanks to the money from the insurance company, her credit card balance was paid off. Which meant she could pick up a few different mediums to play with.

After that she'd stopped at the mall to pick up a pair of shoes, then another stop in Millars Crossing to get groceries.

When she slowed to make the final turn into the ranch her heart skipped, hoping to see Finn again.

"Vancouver is busier than Calgary, isn't it?"

"Way busier." The thought of driving in Vancouver gave her a prickle of anxiety. "My sister lives in West Vancouver and the university is across the inlet, which means bridges, which means traffic and waiting."

"You don't sound too enthused about the idea."

"I'm not."

"Not excited about the driving or not excited about living in Vancouver?"

"Both."

As she spoke the single word, she felt a shift deep within her. And that only added to the struggle she'd been having the past few days. Weeks, if she was honest. Ever since Finn kissed her the first time.

It was as if she had gone through a valley, struggling to get her work done for the program, then was shown, literally and figuratively, a mountaintop. A different choice.

"What are you saying?" He spoke quietly, almost hesitantly.

She waited a moment, weighing what to say, then suddenly was tired of the indecision.

"I wish I was as sure about what I wanted as I used to be." The words seemed to fall out, unfiltered and unchecked. And as she heard what she was saying, she knew it to be true.

At one time her future was clear, but now, as she looked across the porch at a man who had easily captured her attention, and maybe her heart, things weren't as cut and dried as they once had been.

Her conversation with Annie had echoed in her mind all the way to Calgary and back.

"I thought you had a goal?" Finn asked, holding her gaze, his question quiet but ringing in the silence.

Etta looked around the yard. She heard birds singing, wind sifting through the trees. Peaceful, for the most part.

"I thought so too," she finally admitted. "But when I saw the paintings I'd been working on at the restorers, it was the strangest feeling. Like I was looking at someone else's work. I felt like I wasn't that person anymore."

"Do you feel you can go back to painting the pieces you used to?"

This elicited another sigh. Another push of the swing. Another sip of tea as she gathered her thoughts. Sorted through them.

The biggest shift was how she felt about Finn.

"I sent the pictures to the committee just now, which finalized my application," she said, shifting to the topic that lay heaviest on her mind.

"Good."

His single word held an edge, and she guessed it didn't make him happy. Not that she blamed him. She would be foolish if she didn't realize that he was as attracted to her as she was to him. Her application was a commitment to another life. Away from him.

"You don't sound too thrilled about that," she said, feeling as if she was pushing him a bit. Feeling him out.

He set his cup down, walked over to the swing, and dropped down beside her. He took her hands in his and ran his rough fingers over her paint-smeared knuckles. "I'm sticking my neck way out here, but no. I'm not. I want you to stay here."

Etta's heart leapt in her throat as she held Finn's now-serious gaze, his words ringing in her mind and settling in her weary heart.

"I know it's a huge ask, and I'm not a hundred percent sure how things will continue to go with us, but I think it's a safe bet to say we're on a good path. That we fit well together. I'm attracted to you, and I'm thinking you feel the same about me."

She could only nod, her heart now doing some serious pounding in her chest.

"I need to tell you though, before you say anything, that I'm not the kind of guy to play around. I'm getting to the point in my life that anyone I'm involved with, I'll be serious about."

His words created a sense of well-being but, at the same time, a low-level panic. He was laying his heart out, setting everything out for her.

Could she do the same?

She knew loneliness and she knew heartbreak. Her life had seemed empty until she met Finn.

And now?

"You just told me you're going through with your plan to move," he continued. "At least, part of your plan. I don't want you to sacrifice everything for me. I know it's what you want—"

"But that's the thing." She couldn't keep the words to herself anymore. "I don't know what I want anymore." Her gaze clung to his. She wasn't sure what she was seeking, but she felt that somehow he was tangled in the answer to the frantic prayers she had been sending up the past few days.

His gentle smile settled into her soul, evened out the erratic pounding of her heart. He stroked a strand of hair away from her face, tucking it behind her ear, his fingers lingering, touching, connecting.

"I wish I could help you," he said, his voice quiet and even. "I want to be selfish and tell you to stay here, see where this might go, but I can't ask that of you if you're uncertain. I want you to be sure."

She smiled back at him, her own heart feeling as if it knew what it wanted. "I do too."

He smiled and kissed her gently, his lips warm, tasting lightly of salt. He smelled like cut grass and outdoors, and in this moment she felt complete. Whole.

"So, where do we go from here?" he asked.

Etta leaned into him, resting her head in the crook of his neck, feeling the strength of his shoulders. She wanted to stay here forever.

"I talked to my sister. About us."

"Is that a good thing?"

Etta's mind skipped over what she and Annie had talked about. "I tell Annie everything. I told her about us."

"There's an us?"

She chuckled. "I think you know that."

"I do. I'm just glad to know that you do too." He pushed the swing, the rocking soothing her confusion. "What did your sister tell you?"

To tell you everything.

Were they there yet?

She shook the question off and rested her hand on his chest, feeling the slow and steady beat of a heart she wanted to capture wholly and completely.

And in that moment, she felt as if she had one more answer to the questions that had haunted her.

She wanted to be a part of his life. The more time she spent with him, the stronger that feeling became.

"She told me I could probably sell my paintings myself," she said.

"Say what?"

She chuckled at his confusion. "That was her advice when I told her I needed to support myself."

"Could you? Sell your paintings and make a living?"

And that was the question. "I don't know. It takes time to build up a reputation. I would need a place to sell my work."

"Well, there's always the Farmer's Market."

Etta pulled back to see if he was joking. His grin told her he was.

"Sorry. I know this is serious talk," he said. "Besides, you don't want to sell your paintings to a bunch of cheap ranchers. They would need to pay what they're worth."

This made her smile. "They were willing to spend thirty bucks for a sketch."

"Different story, different medium. For fundraisers, the people of Millars Crossing will open their wallets. But to buy something for the house, not so much." He tucked her head back into his neck, resting his head on hers.

She settled against him again, feeling a sense of coming home but still unable to brush aside her concerns.

"Where would you need to sell your paintings?" he asked.

She was grateful to know this was important enough to him to discuss it and, for now at least, take it seriously. "A gallery would be ideal."

"And how do you find said gallery?"

"Ask around. Schlepp my work around. When I was in Calgary, I checked out some galleries. Tried to get a feel of what they like to feature."

"So you were making a plan?"

His question was asked lightly, but beneath that she heard a note of hope.

"Yes. I was making a plan."

He hugged her even tighter. "You have no idea how happy that makes me."

"How about you?" she asked, wanting to shift the conversation from her to him. "Do you have a plan?"

"Yes. I do. I want to settle down on the ranch. I want to get married here, hopefully in Carly's event center, if it ever gets finished. I want to make a life in Millars Crossing and, God willing, have children to teach how to ride and rope and ranch."

She lay quietly in his arms, imagining what that would look like. And slowly, she saw herself coming into the picture.

They sat there, as if absorbing what they had said to each other. Finally Finn drew back, holding Etta's hands, looking deep into her eyes. "I don't know what I'm allowed to think or what I'm allowed to say, but I think we've shared enough for you to know that I'm not dallying around. I want you in my life. I want you to stay here in Millars Crossing if you can make that happen."

She held his gaze, feeling the love he was sharing with her, her own heart softening, yielding to him.

And while she wanted nothing more than to give in to what he was offering, she felt a tiny niggle of doubt. Could she really turn her back on the very thing she'd been working toward so long?

Annie's questions had opened the door to that possibility.

Is that really what you want anymore? Living in the city? Teaching when you love creating so much?

The questions rose up and she knew she had to deal with them. Just as she knew she had to, for her own peace of mind, find a way to support herself.

But lying beneath all of those questions was the one thing

she seemed to struggle with despite all the reassurances she had been given.

Her shame over what had happened with Alistair.

No matter how often Annie told her it wasn't her fault, she couldn't shed her guilt about it so easily.

And she knew she had to tell Finn about it before they went any further in their relationship.

"I hope I can stay here," she said, her hands resting on his shoulders. "I want to make this work." She paused, struggling, then took a deep breath. "And I want us to be sure of what we're doing."

"I couldn't agree more. You need to know that this is important for me because I've already had one bad relationship."

"When?" His words and the frown that appeared on his forehead created a sense of foreboding that she wished she could shake.

"Before I left on my travels. It was a kind of bad time for the family. Everything was falling apart. I was engaged to a woman I thought I loved. I thought I could trust."

Etta felt a shiver trickle down her spine. She held his steady gaze but also felt she was hurtling toward something that could change everything. "What happened?"

"I found out she was cheating on me. With someone who was married." He spat out the last few words like they were the ultimate scandal. "It was bad enough that she broke my trust, but she also broke up this man's family. That was the worst part."

Etta felt as if her shame was written all over her face for Finn to see. She pulled away, icy fingers crawling up and down her spine, chilling her blood and her soul.

"That must have been hard."

"I thought I knew her. Thought I knew who she was. Turned out I was wrong."

Etta swallowed and swallowed, struggling to find her breath.

What was she supposed to do now?

How could she tell him her own truth?

What would he think of her?

Finn stepped out onto the front porch of the house after lunch, and as he walked down the stairs to the ATV parked by the other vehicles, he glanced over at Etta's cabin across the yard.

This morning he had walked over to say hi. To reconnect. But she wasn't in. Carly told him that when she was heading out to the construction site, she had met Etta going for a long hike. Which puzzled him.

Yesterday had been, well, odd, for lack of a better word.

Yesterday he thought he and Etta were headed to a good place. Thought they were in sync. Though he had felt bad about her second thoughts over her future, he was thankful she had her own ideas of settling in Millars Crossing.

Had he scared her off with his declaration?

Last night, after he had told her about Helen, she seemed to retreat again. As he had before, he felt something was going on with her. Something she was holding back.

He shook off the feeling. She was probably tired. He wanted to check in on her. Make sure she was okay.

As he was about to cross the yard, an unfamiliar vehicle pulled in, driving slowly. A small sports car unsuited to driving on the gravel roads of the back country.

B.C. plates, he noticed.

The car parked, and a woman got out. Short. Dark hair pulled back in a sleek bun at the nape of her neck. She wore a tailored suit with a pencil skirt and high heels. She pulled a briefcase out of her car, and when she saw Finn, headed his direction.

Salesperson was the first thing that came to mind.

"Can I help you?" Finn asked, walking toward her.

"Hello. My name is Renate," she said, giving him a polite smile. "I'm looking for Etta Caprice."

"Can I ask what about?" he asked.

"I work for the University of British Columbia. I'd like to talk to Etta about her application."

"Oh. Right. For that teaching job." A flicker of dread trickled through his midsection. Etta had seemed so uncertain.

"Can you tell me where I can find her?"

"I believe she's gone for a hike. I'm not sure when she'll be back."

The woman bit her lip, looking uncertain. "Okay. I've been trying to contact her for a while. I was hoping to connect with her today." She unzipped her purse and pulled out a silver case from which she extracted a business card. Then she got a pen. She scribbled something on the card, then held it out to Finn. "Can you ask her to please, please call me. It's imperative that I speak with her."

"Okay." Finn eyed her plates, then looked back at her. "Will you be around?"

"I'm staying in Millars Crossing at an Airbnb. Apparently, the woman there knows Etta."

Finn released a laugh. "Angie Flikkema knows everybody," he said.

"Well, that's small towns, I guess." She granted him another polite smile, then pointed at the card. "Please make sure she gets that and encourage her to contact me."

She sounded like it was urgent. Finn wondered if she would convince Etta to take the job.

"Okay. I'll do that."

"Thanks. And have a good day." She turned and walked carefully back to her car, got in, and drove away.

Finn flicked the card between his finger and thumb as he watched her leave, tempted to throw the dumb thing away. But he couldn't do that. He couldn't come between Etta and any decision she had to make.

He shoved it in his pocket and hoped he could catch her later this afternoon.

For now, however, he had to check the hay crop. See when they could start baling it.

And try not to get too fussed about the woman's unwelcome visit.

CHAPTER TWELVE

*E*tta was hot and tired when she finally made it back to the ranch. She hadn't meant to walk this far or for this long, but she had lots on her mind and lots to pray about.

As the buildings of the ranch came into view, she breathed a sigh of relief. The trail she had been on was the same one Finn had taken her horseback riding. Of course, it had seemed shorter then. Horses obviously cover more ground in an hour than she could, and she had gotten turned around a couple of times. Though the cell phone reception was spotty, on occasion she got a signal and was able to pull up the compass app on her phone and figure out where to go. Thank goodness the country she walked through was fairly open and she recognized a few landmarks.

But now she was almost at the ranch.

And she had come to a decision.

Yesterday, snuggled up with Finn, talking to him about their future, a sense of hope and expectation had lifted her heart.

Until he told her about his ex-girlfriend. His words were like a knife to her heart.

She had gone to bed last night, sick at heart. She had prayed and read her Bible, seeking guidance. But she already knew what she had to do. She had to tell him about Alistair. If they were to have any kind of relationship, if they were going to move forward, she had to tell him the truth.

And coming to that decision had, surprisingly, brought about a sense of relief.

She had been hiding so long, hiding while she was dating Alistair and hiding from it after. It would feel good to unburden herself.

To a man who had been cheated on?

She had to trust Finn would understand.

With her head held high she strode onto the ranch yard, looking for Finn's truck. It was still parked in front of the house he and Reuben were staying in. But that didn't mean he was on the yard. He had said something about having to check one of the other hayfields to see when they could cut it. He could be out in the fields right now.

She could hear the kids playing and smiled at the sound of their laughter and then Adele's voice calling out to them.

She heard the buzz of the ATV coming from across the yard, from the direction of the hayfields. As it came into view, her heart did that same lift it had for the past while whenever she saw Finn.

He had on a ball cap today instead of his usual cowboy hat. And it looked just as good.

When he saw her, he slowed down, veering away from the shop where he usually parked it, and came toward her.

He waved and she smiled.

And prayed again.

"Hey there," he called out as he parked the ATV by the house and shut it off. He got off and strode toward her.

"Did you have a good hike?" he asked, his hands resting on his waist.

"I did," she said. "Got some great inspiration again."

"This country will do that."

"I saw some really pretty flowers that I might paint."

He chuckled at that. "Now you're talking."

The distance between them bothered her and she took a step closer, taking a chance and resting her hand on his chest. "I'm sorry I've been busy again. But it's good to see you."

It seemed to be all the invitation he needed. He closed the distance between them and pulled her into his arms. "I missed you, girl," he said. He gave her a quick hug then drew back and pressed a quick kiss to her lips.

She rested her hands on his shoulders, holding his gaze, happiness and love flowing through her.

He looked happy to see her, and she allowed herself to bask in his regard.

"I was just going to wash up and then head over to the house to help Katrina. She said she would do supper tonight. Carly is tied up at the construction site."

"I can help too," she said.

"I'm sure you can." He grinned down at her, his smile a white slash against his tanned face. "Oh. Before I forget—" He shifted to pull something out of his back pocket. "Some lady stopped by today and asked me to make sure I gave you this. She wrote something on the back."

Puzzled, she took the business card from him and read it.

And her heart slammed in her throat as she recognized the name on the card.

She swallowed, struggling to breathe through the pounding of her heart.

"What's wrong? You look upset." Finn put his hand on her shoulder.

Etta gripped the card with both hands, trying to still the tremors.

"She said something about talking to you about the job you were applying for?"

She heard the curiosity in his voice but beneath that a note of concern.

"I don't know why. She's not on the board," Etta said, distracted now.

"Who is she?"

And here it was. She had hoped this would happen while they were sitting on the porch, secluded, alone. Not on the yard with the beeping of cement trucks echoing across the space. With the sound of the kids yelling as they chased each other around the house.

"Her name is Renate." Etta wondered if she could go through with this. But she felt again the conviction and behind that her own sister's admonition to come clean. "She's the wife of...of a man I was...I was dating." That sounded better than affair.

Finn's frown and imperceptible retreat made her insides quake.

"What do you mean?"

She sucked in a trembling breath, clenching one hand, the other still holding Renate's card. "She's the wife of the man I told you about. The professor I said was my mentor. Alistair and I dated for about five years. I broke up with him as soon as I found out he was married."

Finn stared at her, his eyes narrowing, his face holding a look of shock that cut her to the core.

"I didn't know," she continued, trying to keep the pleading tone out of her voice. "I had no idea. It was a mistake, and I'm so, so sorry it happened."

But Finn still said nothing, still stared at her as if she was no different than Helen.

And that hurt more than anything.

"You have to believe me," she said.

"This is...this is..." he stammered, shaking his head as if to sort out what she was saying.

She swallowed down a knot of sorrow, fighting the old guilt she thought she had dealt with.

Then she pushed it down and lifted her head, her pride fighting with the shame she had been fighting for the past half year. It wasn't her fault. She clung to the words Annie had pounded into her head, letting them become part of her. "This is hard, I know, but I'm not Helen. I'm not like her. And if you can't accept that, then you may as well leave. Or I will, seeing as how this is your place."

He still stared at her, as if he was trying to figure out what to say.

And that was all she needed.

She turned and went to her cabin. Though she had delivered her ultimatum and walked away, a part of her hoped Finn would knock on the door. Demand to come in. Tell her it didn't matter.

But nothing.

She couldn't stop herself, however. She walked to the window in time to see him striding across the yard as if he couldn't leave her fast enough.

Etta watched, feeling as if her emotions were stretched thinner and thinner with each step he took away from her.

He didn't even look back.

She pulled in a shuddering breath then turned, fighting down the pain of his rejection, struggling to cling to the remnants of pride she had left.

If he couldn't handle the truth then she didn't want him.

But even as she thought it, she knew it was all she could do to not yank open the door and go running after him to beg forgiveness.

Not happening. Though she still struggled with guilt and

regret, she wasn't where she was a few months ago. She believed she was forgiven. If Finn couldn't accept that...

She took a breath and remembered the card Renate had given Finn. With trembling hands she pulled it out of her pocket, almost afraid to turn it over.

Renate had scribbled a note on the back.

Need to talk to you about your paintings.

And under that was her cell phone number.

It took Etta a moment to adjust what she had expected to see to what was actually written there. Every time Renate had tried to contact her, Etta had assumed it was to confront her about Alistair. This was not at all what she expected.

Or maybe it was a way to get in with her seeing as how Etta had been ignoring her calls.

Again, she straightened her shoulders, reminding herself of the comfort she had gleaned from her prayers, from her assurance that her guilt had been washed away. But now, now was her chance to finish this journey.

She pulled out her phone and punched in the number. Renate answered it immediately.

"Hey, Etta. I'm glad you called. I have to apologize for barging in on your private life like I did. I'm sorry if I put you in an awkward spot."

Renate sounded a bit flustered. Not the image Etta had of the woman. They had never met face-to-face but a fellow student had described her as someone who was cool and self-confident.

"I really need to talk to you," Renate said.

"I know." Etta had avoided her long enough. Time to face her past.

Etta maneuvered her car into an empty spot on the streets of Millars Crossing, across the street from Janie's coffee shop. She had suggested meeting Renate here. This time of the day it wouldn't be that busy.

Her heart was pounding, her face hot, but it was time. She had been avoiding Renate long enough. Telling Finn had been one of the hardest things she had ever done, so she figured facing Alistair's wife couldn't be any worse.

As she crossed the street to get to the coffee shop, she saw a woman getting out of a small red car.

Her steps faltered as she recognized Renate.

"Hey there," Renate said, her smile tentative as she joined Etta on the sidewalk.

Which surprised Etta. She was the one who should be uncertain.

"Hello, Renate."

"Thanks for agreeing to meet me," Renate said. She gestured to the coffee shop. "I'm guessing this is where you wanted to talk?"

Etta nodded, hoping and praying it would be empty enough that they could find a quiet spot.

They walked inside and, thankfully, only two of the tables were occupied.

They put in their orders and waited in an awkward silence as Janie made them up. They took their mugs and Etta led them to the back corner.

Renate sat down, blowing out her breath, biting her lip. Then she looked up at Etta. "I'm glad you returned my call."

Her comment surprised Etta. What could she be glad about? She kept quiet, waiting to see where Renate was going. Her own heart was still bruised from Finn's reaction to her news. She didn't want to talk to anyone, let alone the woman whose life she had destroyed.

Renate ran one manicured finger down the handle of her mug, as if gathering her thoughts.

"I'm sure you're wondering why I wanted to connect with you."

Etta was, but kept her silence, not sure what Renate expected of her.

"I need to tell you that I knew about you and Alistair. And I'm sorry to say, his relationship with you wasn't the first time he cheated on me."

Etta's heart stilled in her chest as she struggled to breathe.

"Alistair talked about you at home." She released a short laugh. "He was that confident I suspected nothing. However, from what he said, I gathered you were a young woman of principles."

Her words hooked at her, but Etta kept quiet, giving Renate space to talk.

"I don't know what you thought when you discovered that Alistair was married. I'm guessing, given what Alistair and other people said about you, that you felt betrayed."

"Betrayed and so much more," Etta said, unable to keep quiet anymore. "I felt like an adulteress." She fought to keep her emotions in check. "I couldn't believe… I was stunned…and I'm so, so sorry. When I found out you were leaving him—" She cut herself off, knowing how inadequate her words were.

To her surprise, Renate gave her a gentle smile, her hand reaching out but not touching Etta's. "I believe you. But you also need to know one reason I wanted to talk to you was to tell you that I didn't leave Alistair just because of you. As I said, you weren't the first. With the others, I was willing to look aside for the sake of our children. Until I found out about you. I realized then, with a lot of counseling, that the best way to take care of myself and our sons was to leave him."

Etta still didn't know what to say. She had spent so much time avoiding Renate, struggling with guilt over the repercussions to her family from what she and Alistair had done, that she felt as if her brain was trying to shift into a new gear and grinding its way through the process.

"Alistair cheated on you before?" she asked, latching on to one of the things Renate had said.

Renate held her gaze and gave Etta a wry smile. "Yes."

"When you found out about us…about him and me…" Etta struggled to even admit this in front of Renate.

"I wasn't surprised. Frankly, I was thinking more of you than myself when I found out. You're young, and I knew from things he said that you're incredibly talented. And I know my husband. He can pour on the charm. Make you think you're the most amazing person, the best woman, the prettiest." Renate shook her head, as if to settle her own thoughts. "Sorry. I'm furious with him….and yet…every now and then…"

Trouble was, Etta could relate. "He has a way about him, that's for sure."

Renate released another harsh laugh. "That he does." She pulled in another breath and folded her hands, leaning forward. "You need to know you have no reason to feel guilty about what happened. Please don't take that on. I'm not angry with you. I feel sorry for you. I feel sorry that you had to deal with Alistair. That you had to go through what you did. I don't feel like I have to forgive you for anything, but I know from what I've heard from your fellow students and fellow workers, that you are a caring and principled person. Even though I don't feel you've done anything that needs forgiving, I want you to know that I do forgive you. And I'm saying this for your sake. I don't want you to carry burdens you shouldn't."

As Etta held Renate's gaze, she felt the last weight on her soul ease. Yes, she knew God had forgiven her, but to hear these words of absolution coming from the woman who had haunted her lifted the shadow on her soul, created a happy peace.

If only her heart felt the same.

Once again she thought of Finn. The look of horror she saw on his face when she told him. The subtle retreat and how hard that cut.

"Thank you for that," Etta said, shutting down painful thoughts of Finn. "That means a lot."

They were silent for a few beats, each taking careful sips of tea, as if not sure where to go from here.

Renate put her mug down. "Enough about Alistair. I came to talk to you about something else as well," she said. "Before I married Alistair, I used to run an art gallery with my sister. I loved it. I love discovering new artists, I love finding new things. I know you were applying for an artist-in-residence at the university. I know it's an amazing opportunity, but honestly, I can't see you doing that long-term."

Etta struggled to absorb and sort out what Renate was telling her. "You don't think I could do the artist-in-residence program?" was her first question.

"That's not what I was implying at all. I think you would be fantastic at it, but like I said, I do think you would feel stifled after a while. I've seen your art, and I've seen a slow narrowing of your focus. I know Alistair had a lot to do with that. He loved nothing more than thinking he was shepherding artists toward their real self, when in reality he loved the control he wielded."

As Renate spoke, Etta recognized the truth in her words.

"Your current work is amazing, please don't get me wrong," Renate hurried to assure her. "But I see so much latent talent. Which makes me wonder if you've done anything more? Different?"

"That means a lot, and yes, I have tried other things. Other mediums."

"I would love to see them."

Etta pulled out her phone and scrolled through her photos then turned the screen to Renate.

She looked at them, flicking through the photos, and as she

did, Etta felt a pang of regret that the only record she had of Finn were her sketches and her paintings. No photos.

Because who knew what would happen now?

An icy fist clenched her heart, and she had to swallow to contain the burst of pain it caused.

Would Finn forgive her?

She drew in a deep breath, reminding herself of the forgiveness Renate had just extended to her. The forgiveness she knew God had.

If Finn couldn't get past this...

She didn't want to finish that sentence. Didn't want to think her life had been tossed upside down just when she thought she had found a new direction. Didn't want to think Finn would compare her to his ex-fiancée.

"I have to say, I love your new work," Renate said, expanding one of the pictures, looking more closely, pulling Etta away from her swirling thoughts. "It speaks to me. I know it would speak to a lot of other people as well."

"What are you saying?"

Renate handed Etta her phone back and folded her hands on the table between them. "I'd like to offer you an opportunity to have your work featured at my art gallery. In Vancouver. It's not very well known yet, but my sister has a degree in marketing and has helped another art gallery get off the ground. I'm building an elite clientele who would appreciate your art. If I could feature your work, I could guarantee you it would be of benefit not only to me but also to you."

Etta blinked, trying to understand what she was saying. Trying to place her words in her own scattered and confused thoughts.

"You want to feature my work in your gallery?"

Renate nodded, smiling as if she understood Etta's astonishment. "I know I could do a launch for you worthy of your work. I've been getting some excellent word of mouth. I have about ten thousand followers on my Instagram feed, which would be a great place to tease the public about a showing." Renate leaned forward, her enthusiasm catching. "I know it's a huge switch from where you were going, but I'd like you to give this some serious thought. Though I have to confess I have selfish reasons for hoping you'll go with my offer."

"Would I have to move to Vancouver?"

"Of course not," Renate said with a wave of her hand. "Based on your current work, I can see that you've been inspired by your stay here and I don't want to impede that. However, you would have to travel to Vancouver to deliver new pieces as yours get sold."

Etta sat back, her heart torn. She was being offered an opportunity she would never have considered before. A chance to stay in Millars Crossing.

And at this time? When things were uncertain between her and Finn?

"Let me think about it," she said. The thought of simply producing work held her heart. She knew she could be a good teacher, but the artist-in-residence program was a stepping-stone to something that would be much harder to achieve. A tenured position at the university.

And this way she could live anywhere.

In Millars Crossing?

"You have my card?" Renate asked.

"Yes. I do." She pulled it out of her purse just to make sure. It still held a faint imprint of Finn's dusty finger and her heart hitched at the sight. What lay ahead for them now?

"Excellent." Renate sat back, her smile holding an edge of uncertainty. "I knew it was an enormous risk coming and talking to you. I wasn't sure if you would, but I'm thankful you gave me the opportunity. And I want to let you know that I have been praying for you."

"Thank you," Etta said, returning the woman's smile, still

amazed at how God had worked this minor miracle. "It means a lot to receive your forgiveness."

Renate's smile grew forced. "It took me a while to get here as well, but I know how important forgiveness is and I'm thankful we could talk."

Silence sprawled between them. The quiet that signaled the end of a conversation between strangers.

Etta finished her tea and Renate took her purse and slipped the strap over her shoulder.

"Now that we've talked, I'd like to get back to Calgary. My flight to Vancouver leaves tonight." She pushed her chair back, the metal legs scraping over the tiles, echoing in the now empty cafe.

Etta stood as well and shook Renate's outstretched hand. Renate held Etta's hand just a few beats longer, her eyes holding Etta's. "I just want to wish you well, Etta. I'm glad we could talk."

"Me too," Etta said, granting her a gentle smile. "I was dreading this, but I'm glad it's out of the way."

Renate drew in a quick breath. "And now, I better get going. Take care."

She strode out of the cafe, the bells on the door jangling as it opened then sighed shut behind her.

Etta picked up their mugs and took them to the plastic bin at the end of the counter, avoiding Janie's curious gaze.

She walked to her car and got in, drawing in a deep breath, her emotions in flux.

So much to process.

Burdens had been lifted off her shoulders and now other decisions lay there. On the one hand, working for Renate was a no-brainer. But should she so quickly abandon her own plans? Plans she had been uncertain of, to be sure, but now? After Finn's rejection of her?

She held that thought a moment, her emotions settling and finding their proper place.

She had been honest with Finn. She had told him the truth.

If he couldn't handle it…

What? You'll leave?

She lifted her chin, put her car in gear, and pulled onto the street, headed back to the ranch.

She and Finn needed to talk.

CHAPTER THIRTEEN

"This is the last one," Reuben said, tossing his rope at a cow and calf straggling to catch up to the rest of the herd plodding down the road ahead of them. The cow took another look back, as if longing for the fields she had just been chased out of.

Finn adjusted his seat in the saddle, glad the job was done. It had taken much longer than expected. Thankfully, this bunch of escapees was only a portion of the herd. The damage they had done to Ethan Westerveld's crop was bad enough. Had the entire herd got out, it would have been a disaster.

But oh, Reuben's call had come at a horrible time.

Etta dropped her bombshell on him and he knew he hadn't reacted properly. It had been a huge shock. And then, just as he was about to talk to her, Reuben's text came in.

Their cows were out in Ethan Westerveld's crop, and he was furious. Finn didn't have time to explain.

"I thought that fence would hold them," Finn grumbled, digging his heels in Dancer to make him hurry along. He knew his horse was tired. Dancer was a far superior cutting horse than Reuben's so he and Finn had been working point, moving the cows back along the fence without doing too much further damage to Ethan's canola crop.

"Guess we'll be working on that as soon as we get these critters back," Reuben grumbled. "I thought you had checked all the fences."

"Just the ones in the upper pasture."

"Probably too distracted by the lovely Etta to do a better job."

Finn didn't bother responding to his brother's jibe. The lovely Etta had been far too much on his mind the entire afternoon.

When she'd told him about her ex-boyfriend, his first reaction had been shock. Followed by a very unwelcome anger. Which he had immediately regretted when he saw the look on Etta's face. He wanted to explain. To talk things through, but Reuben's call about the cows had to, unfortunately, take precedence.

He didn't even have a spare moment to call her.

Though the cows had kept him busy, his mind was on Etta's reaction to his reaction. Not only on that, but on the woman who came to talk to Etta. About her paintings.

All the time he and Reuben had been rounding up cows, he wondered if the woman had anything to do with the job Etta had applied for. If she was leaving.

Too much uncertainty, he thought. Maybe they had moved too fast. Hadn't established where they were each going and what they wanted. Maybe he had assumed too much.

But everything had felt so right.

And now?

He sighed. He knew he needed to talk to Etta. Sit down and lay out how he felt and what his hopes were.

If she was still talking to him. He had tried to call her, but she wasn't picking up.

"You look worried," Reuben said. "Wondering what Ethan will do?"

Finn waved that off. "Nope. He's all talk. I think he's just stressed because of his father. I heard he's not doing well."

"I just hope that stress doesn't translate into legal action. Those Westervelds are a force to be reckoned with. Especially Ethan's uncle, Frank."

Again Finn shrugged off his brother's complaint. The Westervelds held less interest for him right now than a woman who had captivated and captured his heart.

He just wished he could find the right way to apologize for his reaction.

The cows were tired after their little rodeo in Ethan's canola and plodded dutifully down the road to the ranch. When they got closer, Reuben rode past them and had the gate to the corrals open by the time the first cow got to the yard. Then he rode back, herding them through the fence.

Finn's heart sank when he topped the rise leading to the ranch and didn't see Etta's car by her cabin.

Was she gone?

Was that all it had taken?

Things were too tenuous for him to assume anything. Expect anything.

And yet the times they had spent together he had sensed a true connection. He had fallen for her. Hard. He thought she felt the same.

They got the cows settled in the corral and Reuben went off to start up the tractor to feed them a bale of hay. That would have to hold them until they got the fence fixed.

Half an hour later Finn banged the last staple into the wire and straightened the kink in his back. The sun was flirting with the horizon and the cooling air was a welcome respite from the heat of the day. All he could think of was Etta, but his phone had died and he knew he had to get this fence fixed before he could do anything else.

Like talk to Etta.

Panic had gripped him while he worked, questions whirling through his head. What if he was too late? What if she had misinterpreted his reaction and left? What if that woman had come to offer the job?

Would she take it?

He could hardly believe she would leave without talking to him.

But why should she when she had bared her soul so completely and he had reacted so poorly?

He dropped the hammer into the pail of staples, set it on the ATV, then started it up and headed back to the yard.

The entire trip back to the yard, he was praying half-formed prayers. Not sure what he could expect or should expect.

And when he came around the barn to park the ATV in the shop, and he saw Etta's car, relief flowed through him.

He didn't even bother to park. Instead, he drove the ATV right up beside Etta's car and turned it off.

Then froze. What was he supposed to say? How was he supposed to breach the topic?

Just be honest. Admit you overreacted.

But even as those words rose up, his pride wanted to beat them down. He had been burnt before. Helen had broken his heart.

Had she? You got over it. And now there's this amazing woman you need to talk to. You need to tell her what's on your heart.

Did he even have the right? Though it wasn't his fault he'd

had to leave right after Etta dropped her bombshell, he could have reacted better.

He sent up a quick prayer for the right words, for the right attitude, then jumped off the ATV and strode to the door.

Just as Etta came out.

She stopped stock-still on the step, her hand resting on her chest, as if protecting her heart. Not that he blamed her.

"I need to talk to you. I need to apologize for my reaction." He couldn't get the words out fast enough.

Etta looked at him, her expression neutral, and his own heart froze.

"I'm sorry," he continued. "I didn't know what to think. What to say. It was a surprise and a shock."

"I'm sure it was." Her voice was quiet. "And I'm not sure what to say back. I've struggled too long to forgive myself, and now I have. Seeing your reaction was hard for me. What happened between me and Alistair was a mistake that I made unintention-ally, and I've been forgiven for it."

He swallowed, not sure what to make of what she was saying.

Though he wanted to defend his actions, he knew he needed to listen.

"Can we go inside?" he asked, not sure he wanted to have this conversation on the front step.

She hesitated, then nodded, standing aside to let him in.

He went straight to the kitchen table and waited for her to join him. She sat down across from him with her hands folded on the table in front of her.

Another prayer, another plea for wisdom and understand-ing, and he pulled the chair out and sat as well.

"So, again, I'm sorry I made it look like I thought your actions were the same as Helen's. That wasn't my intention." He struggled with feeling like he needed to explain himself, however, sensed this was not the time. He saw genuine sorrow on Etta's face, and though he wanted nothing more than to pull her into his arms, to ease it away, he also knew it was not the time for that either. "Tell me about Alistair," he said instead. "If you want to talk about him."

Etta's surprised look gave him some measure of hope.

"I want to hear what you have to say."

She paused, and then, looking away from him, she began.

"Like I told you, he was my art teacher. He gave me a lot of attention when I started attending his classes. I had lost Eli and was feeling vulnerable, and I believe he took advantage of that."

Finn couldn't stop his fists from curling at the thought, but he kept his anger down, his comments to himself. She needed a listening ear.

"I had no idea he was married. I lived a pretty quiet life and kept to myself. Spent most of my time in the university art studio. My roommate was a party girl and was always gone. Of course, Alistair never told me the truth. Why would he?" She released a harsh laugh and again Finn had to fight the urge to comfort her, reassure her.

"Anyway, he strung me along for a few years. Told me we had to keep things quiet, which I understood. I know the policy of profs dating their students. I had tried to break up with him twice, but he kept pleading with me to be patient. Once I graduated we could be more open, he told me. But that didn't change, even when I became his teaching assistant. At any rate, I found out about his wife. Discovered she had left him only a few months before." She released another harsh laugh. "I always thought she left because of me. I felt like an adulteress. Like a homewrecker. It was a low time in my life. In the meantime, I had, under Alistair's encouragement, applied for the artist-in-residence program. A few months after I broke up with Alistair, I found out I was short-listed. That's when I came out here. To work. To forget about what happened."

Finn said nothing, letting his silence show her he was listening. That he had heard her.

Finally he spoke up. "And Renate..." He let the sentence drift off, not sure where she would take the next topic.

"She tried to contact me several times after I left, but I ignored her calls. She even called me one time when I was with you."

Finn remembered that time. Etta's silent retreat. He'd wondered what caused it.

"Why did she come here? To confront you?"

"That's what I thought, but no. She came for a couple of reasons." Another beat of silence as Etta seemed to compose herself. "One reason...one reason..." Her voice faltered, but Finn kept to his side of the table, letting her get through this. She drew in a long breath then squared her shoulders. "She wanted to tell me she'd known about me and Alistair. But that she also knew Alistair hadn't told me about her and their children. That I found out on my own. She wanted to tell me...to tell me she forgave me. That I didn't need to feel guilty about the affair. That I wasn't the first person he cheated on her with. She's left him, but she wanted to assure me that she held nothing against me." She stopped, her fingers resting on her lips as if holding her emotions in check. "Hearing her say that meant a lot to me. I knew I had been forgiven by God, but I also knew that I needed to talk to her. I had thought I would have to ask for her forgiveness, but I didn't think it would be given so easily. It took a huge burden off my soul." Another breath, and this time she turned to him. "I need you to know that as well. I'm not like Helen. I'm not a horrible person—"

"I never said anything like that." He couldn't stop himself now. Her assumption bothered him.

"I poured my heart out to you and you walked away."

Finn stared at her, then shook his head. "No. It wasn't like that at all. I wanted to talk to you, but I got a text from Reuben.

Our cows busted through a fence and were on the loose in our neighbor's canola crop. I had to leave right away. I came back as soon as I could."

Now it was her turn to look dumbfounded. "I thought you couldn't be around me after what I told you."

"No. It was nothing like that. Yes, my reaction wasn't the best and again, I apologize for that. What you told me... surprised me. Wasn't what I expected." He took a chance and reached across the table to take her hand, struggling, praying to find the right words to assure her. "I know you're a principled, unselfish, and sensitive person. I know you would never, ever, hurt anyone deliberately."

Etta held his gaze and for a few heartbeats Finn thought she didn't believe him.

"You left because the cows were out."

Her matter-of-fact statement caught him off guard and all he could do was nod.

"Not because you were judging me."

"I'm not in a position to judge anyone. My life has been such a hodgepodge of bad decisions and choices." Finn kept his hand on the table, close to hers.

"And did you get the cows back?"

This wasn't what he expected to hear, but he nodded.

"I'm glad," she said.

She leaned back in her chair and folded her arms over her chest. "You need to know I've got a lot on my mind," she said. "Lots to think about."

Finn wanted to ask if he would be part of those thoughts but kept his comments to himself, wanting to let her lead the conversation.

"I need some time to myself," was all she said, looking down at the table, ignoring his outstretched hand.

He didn't like this at all, but knew he had no right to push her.

"I understand," he said, struggling with his own emotions and thoughts as he stood. "I'll give you the space you need. But before I go, you need to know that it doesn't matter. What happened before doesn't matter. You mean more to me than any woman ever has and, I'm afraid, ever will."

He waited a beat as if hoping she would look up at him, get up, come over, and melt into his arms.

But she stayed where she was and he turned and left, hope a vague, dimming spark.

You shouldn't have let him leave.

Etta sat at the table, her thoughts a jumble, her emotions uncertain.

Yes, she cared for Finn more than she had cared for anyone. Yes, he was an amazing man who had captured her heart and soul.

But so much had happened in the last while, she knew she had to retreat to catch her breath and her balance. The last time she had fallen for a man, she had been emotionally unstable. She hadn't known what she wanted.

This time, she would be smart. She would give herself space to know her own mind.

And to figure out what to do about Renate's offer.

She walked to her bedroom, sat on the bed, and picked up her Bible. She'd been reading it more and more lately, getting guidance and strength and encouragement from both the Old and New Testaments. And right now, she needed to know what she wanted for herself. Needed to know how she could serve God and be fully her own person.

Curling up on her bed, she opened the Bible to the last passage she had read. Ephesians 20. This passage had resonated as she drove back from Millars Crossing.

"Now to him who is able to do immeasurably more than all we ask or imagine, according to his power that is at work within us..."

Etta placed her finger on the phrase *more than all we ask or imagine* and re-read it. She felt that this was where she had been led the past few days. To a place where she never imagined herself being.

Renate's offer. Her forgiveness and understanding.

But even more, hearing that Finn hadn't judged or rejected her. It had simply been bad timing that he left right after she poured her heart out.

Part of her felt like she should have let him off the hook, but her own reactions were legitimate and she had to acknowledge that.

She returned to the Bible and read the last part of the phrase she had underlined, recognizing once again what was possible for her. God's power was at work within her. God had granted her forgiveness, she knew it in her heart. And Renate's absolution added to the shift she was still adjusting to.

That she was worthy.

She thought of a passage she had read when she first came here. A passage she had a hard time making her own, but now realized the truth and strength of it.

From Matthew. *"The very hairs on your head are all numbered. Fear not, you are of more value than many sparrows."*

Her Lord and Savior was watching over her and saw her as valuable. It wasn't because of what she had done, but simply because of love.

She sat back, still holding the Bible, and stared up at the ceiling as if seeking God.

Then she closed her eyes, prayed for discernment, wisdom, and understanding.

And to do the right thing.

"Have you figured out what to do?" Finn asked Carly as he dried the last pot from dinner that hadn't fit in the dishwasher.

Adele and Wyatt were in the family room playing a game with the kids, and Reuben and Katrina were still out riding in the hills. It was Saturday evening and he hadn't talked to Etta since Thursday.

That very fateful Thursday.

Carly heaved out a sigh. "Not sure. I'm tempted to give my contractor another chance."

"Rather than hire Crossing Construction?"

She clenched her jaw.

"Because that would mean facing Derek, wouldn't it?"

"Make sure you put that pot back in the drawer," was all Carly said. "You put it in the cupboard last time and Adele couldn't find it."

"Those two can't get married soon enough," Finn grumbled. "Then I won't have to worry about what I put where."

"And you would be cooking for yourself in your little house."

"Only until Reuben and Katrina get hitched and move into the house Etta was renting." Carly rinsed out the cloth she had used to wipe the counters and hung it on the tap, pulled the plug, then turned to Finn. "Did she hear anything about that job she applied for?"

"I don't know." Finn didn't mean to sound grumpy, but the past few days had been fraught with tension. He had avoided Etta's cabin as much as possible. Thankfully, he and Reuben were going full-tilt the past couple of days putting up the hay they had cut, so he'd had little time to mope over what was happening or not happening with Etta.

"Did you have a fight?" Carly asked, frowning. "You haven't said anything about her the past couple of days and I haven't seen the two of you together. I thought things were moving along between you."

"They were. Until I messed up."

"How?"

"She told me something about herself and I reacted badly. And then when I was about to apologize, I got a call from Reuben that the cows were out." He wasn't about to give all the details to Carly. It was Etta's secret to share if she wanted.

If she was even sticking around. He had no clue, and it was eating him up inside. But he had promised to give Etta her space, and he was determined to honor that.

"Right. I heard Ethan was underwhelmed."

"Ethan is dealing with a lot of stuff right now." Finn hung the damp towel on the handle of the stove.

"I heard that Sam was sick."

"Probably not going to make it."

"That's sad." Carly was quiet a moment and Finn thought they were done. "And it's sad that I haven't seen you and Etta together. Do you think you can make things up to her?"

"I apologized. She wanted space. This is me, giving her space," he said, pointing to himself. "And now, I'm going back to my cabin and listen to country music and feel sorry for myself."

"You care about her, don't you?"

"I love her. But she has to make up her own mind about what she wants. And I think that's what she's doing right now."

Carly gave him a melancholy smile. "I'm sorry. You two seemed so good together."

"I thought so too. Who knows…" He let the sentence drift away, his hope tethered to it. Then he gave a decisive nod and left.

He let the door fall shut behind him, glancing, as he always did, across the yard at the cabin Etta was staying in. Her car had moved, so she must have gone out today. The light was on, which meant she was still up. Of course, it was only seven-thirty.

He saw the curtain across the window twitch aside, and his heart gave a jump. Was she looking out on the yard? Did she see him?

He shook that off and, as he strode across the yard, he sent up yet another prayer for patience. And a prayer for Etta. That she would find what she wanted. And what she needed. He could imagine that finding out the man she loved was married did a number on her head. He had to allow her to find her own way through that.

But just as he passed the cabin the door opened. He couldn't help himself. He stopped.

Etta stood framed in the doorway, her arms folded over her chest. *Defensive*, he thought, his heart sinking.

"Hey Finn, can we talk?"

He hesitated, not sure he wanted to find out what she wanted to say. She sounded so serious he had a premonition he wouldn't like it.

But he had faced down 1800-pound bulls, avoided deadly hooves, and brought thirteen items through the ten-items-or-less cashier line at Millars Crossing Co-op.

Facing Etta shouldn't be much harder.

Another prayer and another few feet and he stood at the foot of her porch steps.

"Do you have time?" she asked.

"Of course," he assured her, giving her a smile he hoped looked more confident than he felt.

She stood aside as he walked into her cabin. He sucked in a deep breath, willing his pounding heart to slow down.

"Do you want tea or anything?"

"No. I just had dinner at Wyatt's."

"Okay." She stood by the door, her hands twisting around each other, and the faint hope that Finn had nurtured died. "I just want to thank you for giving me the space I asked for. I know it wasn't what you wanted, but it was what I needed." She cleared her throat. "I also need to tell you I got offered the job for the artist-in-residence program."

Finn couldn't breathe. Couldn't think. This was good-bye then.

"But I turned it down."

He blinked, giving his head a shake as if to settle the words she had just tossed at him. "Wait. What?"

"I turned the job down. I got a better, more suitable offer from Renate. When I went to town a few days ago to see her."

Finn wasn't sure which question to toss out first. "More suitable?" was all he could stammer out.

Etta nodded.

"How? Is it in…wherever she's from?"

"I can work from wherever I want. She wants to showcase my work in her gallery. I wanted to have some pieces done for her. Some of the other work I've been doing."

Finn still couldn't seem to wrap his head around what she was saying and why she was telling him.

"But there's one piece I didn't want her to have. I just finished it today." Etta walked over to her easel, which had been facing away from him, and took the canvas off it. It wasn't large. Maybe eighteen by eighteen inches. She looked down at it, smiling, and he wondered what the subject was.

Then she walked over and turned it to him, letting the bottom edge rest on the table so he could see it from the right angle.

It was of him. Kneeling over the calf they had watched being born. The light was soft and the colors were shades of brown and white. A light shone down on him, a pale yellow glow that lit up him and the baby calf curled up in the straw. It was a gentle, moving, painting and, to his surprise, it made him choke up.

"This is how I see you," she said. "Loving, caring, gentle. A man of the land."

"Why did you paint me? I thought you wanted time away from me…" He wasn't sure which question to land on or emphasize.

Etta looked down at the painting, a gentle smile wreathing her face. "I did, but not because I didn't care about you. Because I cared about you too much. And I needed to know for myself who I am and what I want separate from other people's expectations. Including yours. I spent too much time trying to please Alistair, be who he thought I should be, and I wanted to make sure…before…"

Her voice trembled then. She laid the painting down and sat down across from him.

Too far, he thought, but again he sensed she needed this distance between them.

She touched the edge of the canvas. "I painted this as a way of reminding myself who you are and how much you mean to me. When I saw you with that calf, I saw a man at one with the world he was in. I was jealous of that, and yet I felt like it could be my life too. I just wasn't sure how to bring that about. How to put myself in your world and yet be who I was. When I painted this, I knew." She stopped and took a deep, slow breath, as if centering herself. "I can paint what I want, where I want. Renate's offer gives me that opportunity."

Finn could hardly take it all in, not sure he dared follow where she was going for fear he was misinterpreting her.

"I called this painting *Unconditional Love*," she said, looking over at him, holding his gaze, her eyes bright. "When you left, you told me what I meant to you. Even as I clung to those words, I felt that I had to, again, find my way to them. I know who you are, Finn. I see you and I'm hoping, by giving you this painting, that you know how much I see you. How I see you."

He couldn't say anything, the hope he had hardly dared nurture flaring back to life.

"Makes me wish I had spent more time painting," he said, taking refuge in humor. "I could have done one of you, though it wouldn't even begin to show how I feel."

"And how is that?"

He smiled, knowing what she was doing. What she needed.

He took another chance and stood, walked around the table and, taking her hands, tugged her to her feet.

"You're the only person who can, with one smile, make my day better. Who can, with one glance, make me feel like I can do anything. And I would do anything for you. Anything."

"Take painting lessons?"

He chuckled at her reply. "Even that."

"I could teach you."

"I'm sure you could."

He looked down at her, feeling as if his world had shifted into a good, loving place. As if he had finally come home properly. As if he finally belonged somewhere.

"You need to know I'm not leaving."

"That works out good," she said. "Because as long as I can stay in this cabin and paint, I'm not either."

Then Finn pulled her close, and their mouths met in a hungry kiss full of yearning and longing. Their lips moved in harmony, close, touching, soft. Finn wrapped his arms around her and she clung to him. He drew away, ignoring her protest as he gently kissed her cheek, her temple. Then he rested his forehead against hers, thrilling at the feel of her supple body in his arms. Her curves pressed against his.

"You belong here," he said, her face a gentle blur this close. "I don't want you to go. Ever. I want you to stay here. Paint whatever you want. Flowers, horses, mountains, black and white, pink and red. Just please, don't go away from me again."

"I won't. I feel like I know who I am and what I want. What I need." She pressed her hands flat against his back. "And I need you. I want you. Always."

"I like the sound of that," he murmured, pressing another kiss to her welcoming lips. "Stay with me for the rest of our lives. But you need to know you won't have to live in this cabin forever. Someday, I'll build us a bigger place. With lots of rooms for lots of kids. And a huge studio on the top with lots of light for you to work in. Because I see great things coming your way. I know you'll be famous someday."

"I don't know about that."

He released a light laugh. "What? I'm counting on having you take care of me. Of being a kept man so I can start my own artistic career."

"You can do whatever you want, I'm thinking, but for now, let's just leave the division of labor at you working on the ranch and me painting."

"And us, together, planning a wedding."

She pressed her lips together and nodded, her eyes shining.

"Hey, don't cry."

"Hey, don't tell me what to do," she returned with a shaky laugh.

"I think we'll have a lot of fun together," he said, brushing his thumb over an errant tear slipping down her cheek.

"We'll probably have some tears too," she said, growing serious. "Life isn't just sweetness and light."

"I think we both know that well enough. Just think of it as fodder for your creativity."

She chuckled and he pulled her close.

Together. Finally.

If you want to continue your visit to Millars Crossing and find out about Carly and her event's center, find out more here.

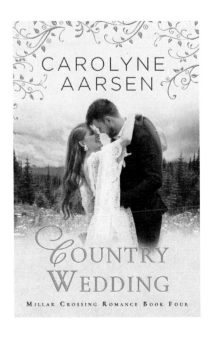

Derek is looking for redemption. Carly is looking to forget.

Once they were engaged and deeply in love, making plans for a future together on her family's ranch. Then an unexpected tragedy and shocking mistakes tore them apart. Derek made the biggest sacrifice of his life and it cost him everything. He also left Carly behind to cancel her dream wedding. She left Millars Crossing, ashamed and humiliated.

Now, years later, Derek is back in Millars Crossing with a desire to move on and create a new start, working with his brother building up their construction company. Carly is back as well and living out a lifelong dream of building an Events Center on the ranch.

When her contractor leaves her in the lurch, Carly is forced to find someone else who can do it before the snow flies.

Unfortunately, Derek is the only contractor she can hire.

Now, forced to work together, they are also forced to face the mistakes and pain of the past.

Can Carly forgive the man who still holds her heart? Can Derek find the forgiveness he needs to truly heal?

Find out more in Country Wedding, the fourth book in the Millars Crossing Romance mini-series.

OTHER SERIES

I have many other books for you to enjoy. Check them out here.

FAMILY BONDS

#1 SEEKING HOME

A rancher who suffered a tragic loss. A single mother on the edge. Can these two find the courage to face a romantic new beginning?

#2 CHOOSING HOME

If you like emergency room drama, second chances, and quaint small-town settings, then you'll adore this romance.

#3 COMING HOME

He thought she chose a hotel over him. She thought he loved money more than her. Years later, can they fill the emptiness in their hearts?

#4 FINDING HOME

She's hiding a terrible truth. He's trying to overcome his scandalous history. Together, forgiveness might give them a second chance.

FAMILY TIES

Four siblings trying to finding their way back to family and faith

A COWBOY'S REUNION

He's still reeling from the breakup. She's ashamed of what she did. Can a chance reunion mend the fence, or are some hearts forever broken? If you like second chance stories, buried passions, and big country settings, then you'll love this emotional novel.

"I enjoyed this book and had trouble putting it down and had to finish it.

If the rest of this series is this great, I look forward to reading more books by Carolyne Aarsen." Karen Semones - Amazon Review

THE COWBOY'S FAMILY

She's desperate. He's loyal. Will a dark lie hold them back from finding love on the ranch? If you like determined heroines, charming cowboys, and family dramas, then you'll love this heartfelt novel.

"What a wonderful series! The first book is Cowboy's Reunion. Tricia's story begins in that book. Emotional stories with wonderful characters. Looking forward to the rest of the books in this series." Jutzie - Amazon reviewer

TAMING THE COWBOY

A saddle bronc trying to prove himself worthy to a father who never loved him. A wedding planner whose ex-fiancee was too busy chasing his own dreams to think of hers. Two people, completely wrong for each other who yet need each other in ways they never realized. Can they let go of their own plans to find a way to heal together?

"This is the third book in the series and I have loved them all. . . . can't wait to see what happens with the last sibling." - Amazon reviewer

THE COWBOY'S RETURN

The final book in the Family Ties Series:

He enlisted in the military, leaving his one true love behind.

She gave herself to a lesser man and paid a terrible price.

In their hometown of Rockyview, they can choose to come together or say a final goodbye...

'This author did an amazing job of turning heartache into happiness with realism and inspirational feeling." Marlene - Amazon Reviewer

SWEETHEARTS OF SWEET CREEK

Come back to faith and love

#1 HOMECOMING

Be swept away by this sweet romance of a woman's search for belonging and second chances and the rugged rancher who helps her heal.

#2 - HER HEARTS PROMISE

When the man she once loved reveals a hidden truth about the past, Nadine has to choose between justice and love.

#3 - CLOSE TO HIS HEART

Can love triumph over tragedy?

#4 - DIVIDED HEARTS

To embrace a second chance at love, they'll need to discover the truths of the past and the possibilities of the future…

#5 - A HERO AT HEART

If you like rekindled chemistry, family drama, and small, beautiful towns, then you'll love this story of heart and heroism.

#6 - A MOTHER'S HEART

If you like matchmaking daughters, heartfelt stories of mending broken homes, and fixer-upper romance, then this story of second chances is just right for you.

HOLMES CROSSING SERIES

The Only Best Place is the first book in the Holmes Crossing Series.

#1 THE ONLY BEST PLACE

One mistake jeopardized their relationship. Will surrendering her dreams to save their marriage destroy her?

#2 ALL IN ONE PLACE

She has sass, spunk and a haunting secret.

#3 THIS PLACE

Her secret could destroy their second chance at love

#4 A SILENCE IN THE HEART

Can a little boy, an injured kitten and a concerned vet with his own past pain, break down the walls of Tracy's heart?

#5 ANY MAN OF MINE

Living with three brothers has made Danielle tired of guys and cowboys. She wants a man. But is she making the right choice?

#6 A PLACE IN HER HEART

Her new boss shattered her dreams and now she has to work with him. But his vision for the magazine she loves puts them at odds. Can they find a way to work together or will his past bitterness blind him to future love.

Made in United States
North Haven, CT
21 January 2022

15055727R00133